AVALon
~ WEB OF MAGIC ~
BOOK 5

Spellsinger

by Rachel Roberts

red sky
PUBLISHING

SCHOLASTIC INC.

NEW YORK TORONTO LONDON AUCKLAND SYDNEY
MEXICO CITY NEW DELHI HONG KONG BUENOS AIRES

Text copyright © 2002 Red Sky Entertainment, Inc.
All rights reserved. Published by Scholastic Inc.
SCHOLASTIC, APPLE PAPERBACKS, and associated logos are trademarks and/or registered trademarks of Scholastic Inc.

"Supernatural High" Written by Debra Davis © 2002 Big Old Soul Music (ASCAP). Lyrics used by permission.

"Take a Chance and Dance," "I Put a Spell on You," "Better," "The Door" © 2002 Fleurdelys Music. Lyrics used by permission.

ISBN 0-439-22170-6

12 11 10 9 8 7 6 5 4 3 2 1   2 3 4 5 6 7/0

Printed in the U.S.A.   40
First Scholastic printing, July 2002

Chapter 1

I'm in my moon phase, my pink days
When everything is okay
I am beautiful, invincible
Perfectly impossible

The music blasted through Kara's stereo, filling her bedroom with the rockin' sounds of Be*Tween. She slid across the polished wood floor, wildly shaking her head of golden hair. Stomping her pink-socked feet to the beat, she spun into a carefully choreographed move and leaped into her closet.

And nothing in this world can shake me
Trip me up or complicate me
Love is all that motivates me 'cause
I'm on a supernatural high

Clothes went flying, piling up everywhere. Kara hopped out, pulling on a pair of jeans and slipping into a blue sweater at the same time. Lyra's spotted head popped out from a mound of clothes as Kara spun past the bed, pulling the cat up by her front paws, sweeping the big animal back and forth.

Kara bent low, feeling the rhythm launch into a wave of guitars and synths. Lyra fell back into a pile of stuffed animals as Kara bounded high into the air, flinging her arms wide. Spinning around, she grabbed her hair dryer and sang into it:

> *I'm a free bird, the magic word*
> *The sweetest sound you've ever heard*
> *I've got a sure thing, a gold ring*
> *I'm wakin' up my wildest dreams*

Against the windowsill, Lyra lay on her back in the middle of Kara's stuffed audience. Kara dove into the fluffy mountain and tickled the cat's belly, causing Lyra to yelp as they both sang along with their favorite new band:

> *And nothing in this world can change it*
> *Turn me around or rearrange me*
> *Love is all that matters lately 'cause*
> *I'm on a supernatural high*

Kara was multitasking — dressing, dancing, singing, and celebrating all at the same time. She was so cool — life was so cool. Since she had received word that Be*Tween would play at the Ravenswood Wildlife Preserve benefit concert, Kara had been pumped, playing the CD nonstop. No one believed she could really pull this off. But she had stayed focused and determined, stationing herself at Town Hall every day for the past two weeks. A barrage of E-mails and a phone call from her dad, Mayor Davies, had convinced Be*Tween's manager that the popular girl band could make a stop in Kara's town, Stonehill.

She danced over to her desk, stuffed a stack of papers into her new briefcase, and snapped it closed. When she put her mind to something, there wasn't anything she couldn't do. And for the first time since Kara had convinced her dad to let her, Adriane, and Emily become tour guides for the preserve, the council actually seemed excited. All except Mrs. Beasley Windor, who had made it her personal task to keep an eye on the girls. Mrs. Windor had wanted the old manor house torn down and the land redeveloped into a country club and golf course. But thanks to Kara, this was going to be the event of the year and it would be Ravenswood — 1, Windor — 0.

Outside, a horn honked. Kara turned to Lyra. "It's show time!"

"Already?" Lyra peeked out from behind the bed where she had toppled onto a comfortable pillow.

Kara heard the cat's voice in her mind. At first, it had felt odd, but now it was like second nature, as if she and the magical cat had been best friends forever.

She opened the big window over her desk. "I'll see you at Ravenswood."

Lyra leaped to the windowsill, brushing her face against Kara's. *"Later."*

"Love you." Kara gave the cat a quick kiss and ran for the door.

She took the stairs two at a time. "Mom! I'm going! Dad's taking me over to Ravenswood."

"Okay," Mrs. Davies called from her study. She sounded preoccupied; she was probably working on another big divorce case or looking up case studies.

Kara shot out the front door, bolting into a crisp October morning.

"Are you okay?" Lyra peeked out from behind a hedge.

"Of course. Go before my dad sees you," Kara called out as the big cat slunk into the woods bordering the Davies' property. A golden glow ran up and down the cat's spotted back as two large wings unfolded.

"And don't let anyone see you flying!"

"Cats don't fly." In a moment, Lyra was soaring

over the Chitakaway River and into the dense woodlands beyond.

Kara ran across the front lawn to the dark green Lexus waiting in the driveway. She hopped into the passenger seat, popping down the sun visor to check her hair in the mirror. "Hi, Daddy."

"All ready, princess?" The handsome mayor of Stonehill smiled, running fingers through his graying but thick hair.

"I have all the papers right here." She smiled, showing off her new leather case, a gift from the mayor's staff. They'd been very impressed with the diligence of Ravenswood's young president. At least *some* people appreciated her efforts.

"You still have to get final approval from Mrs. Windor and the rest of the Ravenswood committee for the construction of your stage," Mayor Davies reminded her, pulling the car out of the driveway.

"No prob, Mayor Davies. Everything's under control."

❧   ❧   ❧

Mrs. Beasley Windor tapped her foot impatiently, beady eyes darting back and forth. She raised the large lion's head door knocker and pounded away at the front door to Ravenswood Manor. A few members of the council were with her, including Sid Stewart, Lionel Waxxer, and

Mary Rollins. While they waited, they looked out over the front lawn toward the sculpture gardens.

"We haven't seen anything unusual so far, Beasley," Sid remarked.

"Just keep your eyes open," Mrs. Windor said, scanning the thick woods that bordered the property. "Something strange is going on out here, and I'm going to find out what."

"Hoo doo yoo doo."

Startled, Mrs. Windor spun around. Emily walked across the gravel driveway toward the group. A great snow owl was perched on the girl's shoulder. The owl's flared wing tips sparkled with flecks of turquoise and lavender. Mrs. Windor eyed the owl suspiciously. She could have sworn the owl just spoke. No one else seemed to have heard anything unusual. But the girl, Emily . . . did she just give that bird a warning look?

"Hi, everyone," Emily said, quickly stroking the owl's wings closed. "Er . . . Kara's on her way, and Adriane must be in the library at the computer."

"Hello, Emily. We hear your Ravenswood Website has gotten quite a few hits," Sid Stewart said.

Emily smiled. "It's getting really busy! We've linked to the kids' division of the National Humane Society called NAHEE. It's all about helping animals."

6

"Very interesting," Mary Rollins said, clearly impressed.

"Yes, and our teacher is giving us extra credit for sharing it with the school." Emily looked at Mrs. Windor. "I'd be happy to show you —"

"I want to see everything!" Mrs. Windor snapped. "And I want a list of every animal here on the preserve. Every since that *peculiar* incident at Miller's Industrial Park, animals have shown up at the mall and even at the school. Your disruption at the football game with that — *horse* thing was too much!"

Emily winced, thinking about the unicorn, Lorelei. Emily had felt such a strong bond with her, and although the unicorn had been gone for only a few weeks, Emily missed her greatly. "We thought the Stonehill Sparks could use a mascot. It would tie into the whole theme of Ravenswood Preserve being such an important place for animals."

"You're saying a *unicorn* represents the theme of Ravenswood?" Mrs. Windor snarled.

"No . . . it's just . . ."

"Oh c'mon, Beasley," Sid chuckled. "It was just a make-believe unicorn. Very imaginative, too."

"And the kids loved it," added Lionel.

Mrs. Windor glared at Emily. "Just what kind of

animals are you hiding here?" she asked accusingly.

From the corner of her eye, Emily caught Lyra dropping from the skies behind the manor.

"Just the ones that live here . . . I mean —" she sputtered nervously.

"We do have a deal with the Town Council, if you remember, to protect *all* the animals that live here," said a new voice.

Everyone turned as Nakoda Chardáy, Adriane's grandmother and the official caretaker of Ravenswood, emerged from the front door of the manor house. "In the absence of the owner, Mr. Gardener, the girls have done a wonderful job managing Ravenswood."

"Our *deal* is to see if the preserve makes economic sense for the town," Mrs. Windor countered.

"And we're willing to open the preserve for the benefit concert," Gran reminded her. "With a percentage of the profits going to the Stonehill Council."

"Assuming there *are* profits," Mrs. Windor said. "You're asking us to pay for some rock-and-roll concert when this land could be put to a real benefit for everyone."

"Tourism dollars are the backbone of many small communities," Lionel mused.

"You'll see," Emily said. "It's going to be great."

"It's not going to *be* anything at all, young lady," Mrs. Windor reminded her. "Not until *we* say it is."

The mayor's Lexus pulled into the wide circular driveway and came to a stop. Kara bounded out. "Hey, kids!"

"Ah, Mayor Davies," Lionel said as he walked to the mayor to shake his hand. Sid was right behind him.

"Greetings, Sid, Lionel, Mary. A beautiful day, isn't it, Beasley?"

"Mayor Davies," Mrs. Windor said gruffly, wagging her finger. "I expect a complete breakdown of this proposed event."

"Right! I have all the specs right here." Kara flipped her hair back and opened her briefcase.

"Good day to you, Mrs. Chardáy." The mayor bowed to Gran and turned to face Mrs. Windor. "Kara has it all worked up, Beasley," he said.

Kara smiled and glanced down at the papers and gasped. They were all out of order!

Emily slid in with a save. "Come on, we'll show you where the event will take place out on the great lawn."

Shuffling papers, Kara followed Emily as she herded the group along the path that led to the magnificent back lawn bordered by wondrous gardens. The surrounding trees were ablaze with the colors of autumn.

A sudden rustling made Mrs. Windor look around furtively. Something with soft blue-and-pink fur danced past the trees.

"The stage will go there," Kara pointed out quickly, managing to draw Mrs. Windor's attention away from the magical animals that should have been safely hidden. *That is supposed to be Adriane's responsibility,* Kara thought, annoyed.

"The stage is really just a raised platform," Mayor Davies added. "The show goes on from four till six, Saturday afternoon."

Kara finished sorting out the papers. She held them out to Mrs. Windor. "It's all right here."

Mrs. Windor glared at Kara as she took the papers.

"With the newest, hottest band coming, it's sure to be a hit!" Kara exclaimed.

"Not exactly."

The group whirled around. Adriane walked toward them, a paper fluttering in her hand. "Be*Tween isn't coming."

"What?" Kara ran over to her.

"Look for yourself." Adriane held up a printout. Kara snatched the E-mail.

Dear Miss Davies,
Unfortunately, Be*Tween will not be able
to make an appearance at your benefit

concert. Their entire tour has been can-
celed due to unforeseen events. We hope
this does not interfere with your plans and
we regret the inconvenience.
Joseph Blackpool, CEO
Cigam Management

"Be*Tween isn't coming?" Kara repeated glumly,
all the energy draining out of her.

"Well, there goes your little show," Mrs. Windor said with a smirk.

"No way!" Kara said, trying to think fast. "They
have to show up!"

"They're missing," Adriane said.

"Huh?"

"Word on the Net says Be*Tween vanished.
Just disappeared."

"Disappeared? How does a group like Be*Tween
just disappear?" It was probably all part of some
bogus publicity stunt, to get people talking. And
who cares about some little benefit concert, right?
Kara kicked a small stone. "That's just great!"

"However . . ." Adriane said with a sly edge to
her voice.

"What?" Kara was almost afraid to ask.

"There's a second E-mail." Adriane's dark eyes
twinkled as she held up a second printout.

"What? What?!" Kara grabbed for it.

"Let's see here . . ." Adriane teased her, moving the paper out of Kara's clasping fingers.

"Hurry up! Oh, give me that!" Kara grabbed the E-mail.

> Miss Davies,
> Further to our last E-mail, we received notice that one of our premier musical performers has volunteered to personally replace Be*Tween at your benefit event: Johnny Conrad.

Kara's eyes went wide.

"Johnny Conrad . . ." Kara wobbled and sank to the ground. "Johnny Conrad . . . coming here!" she screamed.

"Johnny Conrad? Even I've heard of him!" Mary Rollins exclaimed.

"Wow! He's one of the biggest stars in the world!" Emily said, amazed.

Kara jumped to her feet. "Johnny Conrad is coming here!" She swooned and promptly sat down again.

"Can you believe it?" Adriane grinned. "This town is going to rock!"

"*Ahhh!*" Kara screamed.

Emily and Adriane screamed.

The three girls were hugging and jumping up and down together.

"Well, I would say this is an event sure to generate some publicity for Ravenswood," Mayor Davies smiled. "Good work, girls."

"Johnny Conrad!" Kara squealed, stomping her pink sneakers into the grass.

Sid pulled Mrs. Windor aside. "Do you know what kind of crowd a star name like that will attract?" he whispered. "Thousands of people are going to show up!"

"Yes . . ." Mrs. Windor smiled. "Think of it, thousands of kids, press, and tourists all coming here to the Ravenswood Preserve."

"This will surely put Ravenswood on the map," Sid said proudly.

"If there's anything left of it after it's over," Mrs. Windor whispered, grinning.

Chapter 2

beachbunny: have you heard the l8est?

irishrose: 4sure, Be*Tween's the greatest

swandiver: they've got every new band beat

beachbunny: no one can compete

Sunlight poured through the large round windows of Ravenswood Manor's library, gently caressing Kara's face as she watched the messages flying in the Ravenswood chat room. With the buzz of Be*Tween coming to town, the number of visitors had risen considerably. Drawing a deep breath, she let her fingers dance over the keyboard.

kstar: got some news today — Be*Tween can't come and play

chinadoll: :-! what happened?

swandiver: :-(what's wrong?

irishrose: I just heard their latest song

beachbunny: they didn't break up, did they?

irishrose: =^..^= tell me that's not what u'r gonna say

For an instant, Kara considered admitting the band's disappearance, but the truth was, Kara had no idea what was *really* going on with Be*Tween. She'd learned to be careful about believing a lot of stuff people posted on the Net.

kstar: fear nottest, we got the hottest

irishrose: who could be so cool?

beachbunny: we must tell everyone at school

kstar: Johnny Conrad!

swandiver: Johnny Conrad? I'm screamin! :-O O-:

irishrose: that's incredible!

chinadoll: he's so hot!

beachbunny: Johnny Conrad! i must be dreamin!

A sudden tap on the shoulder made Kara jump half out of her skin. "Hey, Britney!"

"What?" Kara snapped. She whirled around to see Adriane standing behind her with a grave expression.

"We got a problem," Adriane said. "It's Mrs. Windor. She came in with the construction teams."

"So? Let her boss them around for a bit. Give her something to do."

"She's snuck off into the woods. She's out there right now and she's got a camera."

Kara's stomach tightened. "Did you get the feeling that she caved too easily on this concert?"

"Yeah, it had crossed my mind," Adriane said.

"Let's go!" Kara exclaimed.

Logging off, Kara and Adriane raced from the library, down the rear stairs and out the back of the mansion. About ten men were hauling huge planks of wood across the great lawn. Another group rolled cable and equipment. Others stood looking at a set of plans.

"Where is she now?" Kara asked Adriane.

"Storm, what's happening?" Adriane called into empty air. Instantly, she heard the silver mistwolf's answer in her mind. *She's headed for the Rocking Stone.*

Kara heard, too. "Oh, great! What if she finds the glade?" Kara hissed. "What's Storm going to do? Wrestle Mrs. W. to the ground and take her camera? That would look really good!"

"That's why you're here," Adriane smirked. "We need some presidential action."

They flew past the hedge maze toward the woods. Only a small barrier of trees separated the giant Rocking Stone boulder from the magical glade where so many of the homeless animals from the magic world of Aldenmor lived.

Mrs. Windor was determined to shut down Ravenswood through any means necessary, and if she could show the Town Council pictures of strange creatures — or even what looked like bizarre animals — running loose in the preserve, she'd almost certainly get her way. And that would only be the start of the trouble they'd all face. If scientists or some other government agency examined any of the magical animals at Ravenswood, the truth would be discovered and they would remain in cages, possibly the subject of experiments — or worse — for the rest of their lives.

They could not let that happen to their friends. Frowning, Kara and Adriane ran into the woods.

❧   ❧   ❧

Beasley Windor nearly tripped a half dozen times on roots she could have sworn were trying to snag her. She had whacked her head twice on low-lying branches that she was certain swept in at her out of nowhere — it simply couldn't have been that she was looking one way and walking another. This was a dangerous place.

It had to go.

Giggling and whispers floated through the woods.

Who was that?

More giggles followed, then a flutter of leaves

made Mrs. Windor turn to a large outcropping of willow trees. She carefully tiptoed off the trail.

Slightly hunched over, she peered into the small square of the digital camera she had borrowed from her niece.

Strange creatures were here, and they were playing games with her. They were certain they had nothing to fear — and that belief would be their undoing.

"I've got you now," she whispered.

🌀   🌀   🌀

"She's moving away from the glade," Kara whispered. She couldn't believe their luck —

Adriane gasped, pointing. "Right into trouble."

Kara and Adriane hid behind a tree, watching as Mrs. Windor walked directly toward a space between two bushy willow trees where a pack of quiffles waited. The strange, ducklike creatures were holding a large tree branch pulled back tight, ready to let it fly at their unsuspecting visitor. Their big, webbed feet tapped silently with anticipation and they kept looking up to steal glances at the woman moving in their direction.

"We've got to do something!" Adriane said urgently.

"We can tell her they're migrating visitors from Canada," Kara suggested.

"Uh-huh, and what about that?" Adriane pointed behind the quiffles. "A visitor from Atlantis?"

Kara's eyes widened. Standing a dozen feet beyond the quiffles, in a pool of warm golden light, stood a pony with green-and-purple wings — a pegasus. All Mrs. Windor had to do was turn to the right with her camera and she would get the video of the year.

"Do something!" Adriane pushed Kara.

"All right, all right. You create a diversion with your jewel." Kara pointed to the golden wolf stone locked in the black band around Adriane's right wrist. "I'll take care of Mrs. Windor."

Boldly, Kara stepped out from behind the tree. Behind her she heard a faint crackling and felt magical power building. Turning sharply, she saw Adriane snap into a fighting stance, whirling her arm in a circle. The wolf stone glowed brightly with sparkling energy.

"On second thought —" Kara said, reaching out to Adriane, but she was too late. A searing bolt of golden light ripped from the stone, smashing into a cluster of dead branches over Mrs. Windor with a terrible explosion.

Whammm-crrrackkkk!

Three quiffles went flying as the branch shot forward. Mrs. Windor shrieked and all but flung the

camera away. She whirled toward the opening —
where a collection of seared branches crackled down,
quickly piling up to obscure her view of the pegasus.

Kara gave Adriane a stern look.

"You said create a diversion," Adriane said innocently.

"I didn't say to knock down the whole forest!"

A small blur of gold-and-brown fur dashed behind the new barrier, kicking the magical animals
away, herding them deeper into the wilds of
Ravenswood. Kara breathed a sigh of relief as she
saw Ozzie, the magical ferret, give her a thumbs-
up — well, actually a paws-up.

Mrs. Windor was frantically whirling in every
direction, rocking on her heels as if she had just
made herself dizzy.

"Who's out there?" Mrs. Windor hollered.

Kara and Adriane ducked back behind the
cover of the wide tree trunk.

Something rustled through the trees again.

Mrs. Windor began shouting. "Come out of
there, right now!"

Kara and Adriane poked their heads out from
either side of the tree just in time to see Mrs. Windor about to trip over Rommel the wommel!

"Get out there and get rid of her!" Adriane said
as she pressed her back against the tree trunk.

"Okay, okay. And no more magic!"

"Right."

"Hey, watch where you're —!" Rommel started, but his warning came too late.

Mrs. Windor, still holding onto the camera with pale, trembling fingers, looked into the face of the small, talking koalalike bear. She leaped back, cried out, and tripped, landing in a patch of mud and muck.

By the time she raised her camera and wiped the lens clean, Rommel had rushed off.

"I've got you!" Mrs. Windor shouted, spitting out muddy goop.

"Oh, no," Kara said. What were they supposed to do now?

A sudden gust of wind blew around the woman, a spiral of force that kicked up mud and earth and stone, quickly forming what looked like a mini-twister!

"Adriane!" Kara hissed. "Stop it!"

The dark-haired girl looked at her wolf stone. The jewel was pulsing with strong amber light. "I'm not doing that!"

Then the ground beneath Mrs. Windor trembled. The circling winds drew closer to the struggling woman.

Suddenly, Mrs. Windor's camera was ripped from her hands by the winds. It flew into the air, smashing into pieces as it hit a hard, flat stone.

"What are you *doing*?" Kara yelled.

Adriane threw up her hands. "It's not me, it's not me!"

Next to Mrs. Windor, the whirlwind picked up earth and stone, grass and vine, twigs, branches, leaves, and more dirt, magically forming into a round, tumbleweed shape.

The wind settled, but within its "body," the elements continued to ebb and flow. Sticks, dirt, and leaves swirled.

"It's an earth Fairimental!" Adriane gasped.

Fairimentals were extremely magical beings, the keepers and protectors of good magic on Aldenmor.

"What's it doing here?" Kara asked.

"Warrriorrr," the tumbleweed rumbled, bits of leaves and dirt flying as it wobbled about.

"What the —?" Mrs. Windor looked closely at the twirling mass.

With a sudden shudder, the Fairimental exploded, sending fragments of debris everywhere.

Mrs. Windor whirled around and raced back through the woods, howling.

Adriane and Kara ran to the various pieces of the Fairimental. Two tiny whirlpools of dirt and leaves spun from the ground, desperately trying to regain shape.

"Warrior," one said. Rattling crazily, the whirlpool flew apart.

"We need help," the other small pile managed to say. It, too, was starting to break up.

"What's happened?" Adriane asked urgently.

"— protect Avalon — blazing star must — careful —" words rushed forward, broken like pieces of earth flying from the creature's magical form.

"Spellsing as three — whatever — will be —"

Then whatever force was holding the Fairimental together abruptly vanished, and its elements crumbled to the ground.

Adriane looked at Kara.

The girls knew that the Dark Sorceress of Aldenmor would stop at nothing to find magic. Avalon was the legendary source of *all* magic. Her most recent attempts had damaged the magic web itself, the strands of magical energy that connected worlds everywhere, and supposedly reached all the way to Avalon. As far as the girls knew, the portals to the fairy glen on Aldenmor — where the Fairimentals lived — were still missing. No one had seen or heard from the Fairimentals since those portals had disappeared . . . until now.

"We have to tell Emily about this. The Fairimentals need our help," Adriane called to her.

Kara shot her a withering gaze. "Well, that's

your department, isn't it? Saving the day? I just have my stupid little concert to take care of, thank you very much!"

She walked off, head held high.

"Wait!" Adriane ran after her. "It said you had to be careful."

"It's a twig!" Kara yelled. "It was hard to understand anything it said."

"We have to get a message to Zach," Adriane insisted, referring to the human boy she'd met on Aldenmor who'd been raised by mistwolves.

Now Kara tossed her hands in the air. She spun back to face Adriane. "And how do you propose we do that?" she yelled. "We've got Mrs. Windor running around and Johnny Conrad is arriving in two days! We can't have Fairimentals and who knows what else popping up! And now you want a long-distance dragonfly phone call to Aldenmor. That's the *last* thing I need right now!"

Adriane had to agree with Kara on that one. "Maybe we should just postpone the benefit," she suggested quietly.

"No *way!*" Kara insisted. "This show is going on! The Fairy Glen and Avalon are just going to have to wait."

Chapter 3

Emily raced up the steps of Stonehill's Town Hall. It was a little after four on Thursday, and hundreds of people were gathered on the sidewalk facing the old redbrick building. Main Street had been cleared of parked cars and blocked off, and the park across the street from the Town Hall was filled with even more spectators. Photographers and people with video cameras — including professional TV news crews — had descended upon the normally quiet town square.

At the top of the steps, near the front entrance, stood a small podium with a microphone stand. A WELCOME JOHNNY CONRAD banner fluttered.

A pudgy security guard with curly red hair and freckles stood beside the main doors. "Hello, Emily. Got quite a crowd today."

"Hey, George!" Emily said breathlessly as she slipped past him. She flew down the dark wood-paneled corridor, passing dozens of photographs detailing Stonehill's history. She whipped past an

25

open door where she smelled food and heard laughter. Inside, Mayor Davies and the Town Council gathered in the small room, chatting.

The real activity was centered in the main meeting room. Emily burst through the doors and was nearly run over by Kara's brother, Kyle, and his friend Marcus, who were rushing by with stacks of folding chairs in their arms. The meeting room had been transformed into a reception hall, complete with streamers strung across the walls, balloons bouncing above wide, neatly decorated tables, and a budget-busting buffet piled with enough food to satisfy the entire population of Stonehill — twice!

"Over to the left . . . a bit higher," Kara commanded, standing in the midst of her "troops," more than two dozen volunteers from school. Her buddies Heather, Tiffany, and Molly were doing their best to center a big poster of Johnny Conrad on the rear wall.

"It looks great, Kara!" Heather yelled.

"My arm is getting sore!" Molly muttered.

"No pain, no party!" Kara hollered. She looked down and brushed the front of her new blue sweater, one eyebrow raised defensively at the possibility of a stray crumb.

Emily approached slowly and cautiously. "Hi. My name is Emily. Can Kara come out to play?"

Kara slumped against the door. "I'm acting like a witch, aren't I?"

"Are you a good witch, or a bad witch?"

"Very funny." Kara sighed. "There's just so much going on. . . ."

"You're doing a great job," Emily reassured her. "And so is everyone else. It would be nice if they heard that now and then."

"Yeah." Kara looked away. "Um . . . is Adriane coming?"

"Are you kidding?" Emily exclaimed. "This is Johnny Conrad!"

"What do you think we should do about the Fairimental's message?"

"We should contact Zach after the press conference, when everything calms down — whenever you're ready," Emily answered.

"The last thing we need are those dragonflies popping up! I'll never get rid of them."

Something *squawked* in Kara's bag. She hauled out a small walkie-talkie.

"Ground control," she said.

"Drone One to Queen Bee," a voice hissed.

"Go ahead, Drone One."

"Target spotted. Headed right toward Main Street. You are not going to believe it!"

"Stay calm, Drone One . . ." Kara urged.

"It's Johnny *Conrad*! *Ahhhh!*" The walkie-talkie crackled and cut off.

"We've lost Drone One," Kara said. She quickly checked her watch. "T-minus five and counting. How do I look?" She fluffed her blond hair.

"Perfect."

Kara grinned. "Let's move out!"

They ran into the room where her father and the other council members were still chatting away.

"People! People!" Kara hollered. "Let's go. Our guest of honor has arrived!"

"Ooo, how exciting," Mary Rollins exclaimed.

"Let's keep this orderly now," Mayor Davies stated. "Just another visitor to our humble town."

"Look! It's Johnny Conrad!" Heather was jumping up and down, pointing out the front window.

"*Ahhhh!*" Tiffany screamed.

Everyone in the room rushed for the door at once, squashing the mayor to get past him. Soon the vast crowd outside started screaming.

This was it. Kara was about to become a star.

❧   ❧   ❧

Outside the Town Hall, Kara stood beside her dad. She heard the rumble of engines and the blare of car horns.

And in the distance . . . music?

Kara's eyes widened as she and everyone else in the enormous crowd turned toward the street, where a jet-black convertible T-Bird with the top down drifted their way. A young, dark-haired guy stood on the front hood, a microphone in his hand. A tour bus crept along at a respectful distance behind the singer. Two huge speakers hung on either side of the T-Bird, and a guy with black sunglasses sat with a mixer board in the back while another one drove, their heads bobbing to the beat of the thundering, pulsating, blisteringly happening song that was currently topping the charts.

Let me tell you, if I sing it true, get up and start the dance,
A rock-and-roll rap with some zap, come on now and take a chance,
No matter what you do, it's your life, you're you,
So come on and take a chance and dance!

Johnny Conrad's thick, tousled black hair glistened in the golden afternoon sunlight and the deep, model-perfect cheekbones filled with dusky shadows as he rapped. His soulful deep blue eyes were cast heavenward, and his lanky muscular body swayed with the music, his pale shirt clinging, his black leather boots and pants shining as his long leather jacket curled behind him. The booming music seemed to ensnare his listeners as everyone moved to the beat. Molly, Heather, and

Tiffany were bopping like crazy, dancing around the black car as it rolled up to the curb.

DANCE! DANCE! DANCE! TAKE A CHANCE AND DANCE!

The entire crowd was caught in the rhythm, the enveloping sounds, and the enchantment that was Johnny Conrad. Dancing, moving, shaking, and screaming, adults, teens, and children all rocked out to the sounds of the latest teen sensation.

Johnny leaped from the hood, his wireless microphone catching every note as he sang his heart out. Security held the crowds back as Johnny climbed the wide steps of the Town Hall, heading right for the podium, while constantly turning, reaching out, his soulful eyes connecting with as many people in the crowd as he could.

The song ended and Johnny took a bow, prompting another round of searing screams from his audience. Smiling, he waved and tossed the microphone to his driver.

Mayor Davies stared in slack-jawed wonder at Johnny, who patiently nodded and waved to his fans — and the press. Cameras flashed, bursting bright lights against the singer's brilliant blue eyes.

"Hello, Stonehill!" Johnny called out.

The crowd erupted in frantic, ear-piercing screams. "Johnny! Johnny!"

Kara was practically beside herself as the superstar approached. But she had a job to do, so she nudged her dad's arm, snapping him to attention. She noticed Adriane next to Emily, jumping and cheering.

Mayor Davies cleared his throat four times, right into the podium's microphone, but nothing happened until Johnny put a single finger to his lips and winked at the adoring crowd — which suddenly fell completely silent.

"They're all yours," Johnny whispered, nodding to the mayor.

Kara watched Johnny, transfixed.

Whoa. This guy was *hot*.

"Johnny Conrad, thank you for taking time out of your busy schedule to help Ravenswood Wildlife Preserve — your act of generosity has moved us all," Mayor Davies read from the script Kara had written. She nodded, smiling ear to ear. "The Town Council would like to offer you and your band our best suites at the Stonehill Inn. And as mayor of Stonehill, I'd like to present you with the key to our city!"

Covering the microphone, Mayor Davies nodded toward Kara, "I think you've already won the key to my daughter's heart."

"Dad!" Kara wailed.

Johnny smiled at Kara — and she managed not to faint. Then he turned to the crowd and shot them a dazzling smile, holding the big golden key high over his head.

"Thank you very much. We're proud to play for the wonderful cause of the Ravenswood Preservation Society." He winked at Kara.

Kara practically leaped into the air, but instead hopped around and screamed like a starstruck little girl.

"And we've got something really special planned," Johnny said. "As part of a promotion for my new CD, *Under Your Spell* —"

Screams broke the speech, but quieted down as Johnny raised his arms.

"I'm hereby inviting one fan to sing onstage with me during the concert Saturday. The performance will be simulcast via the Internet all over the world!"

"*Ahhh!*" Kara screamed.

"*Ahhhhh!*" dozens of girls screamed with her.

"*Ahhhhhhhh!*" the crowd screamed and screamed and screamed some more.

Sid Stewart put his hands over his ears, screaming in pain.

"That's right, I'm offering a place for one special person to sing with me . . . if I can only find him . . . or her." Johnny eyed Adriane, who blushed but smiled back. Then he looked at Emily. And then, suddenly, Johnny zoomed in on Kara and seemed to see . . . something. "Maybe I already have."

Kara's heart skipped a beat.

He means me, she thought. *Yes! He's talking about me!*

Kara struggled to control herself. She took a step toward the microphone and was about to speak when Adriane stepped on Kara's foot and took the mike. "I'd like to invite you and the band to stay at Ravenswood Manor," she quickly said, holding the mike away from Kara's grabbing fingers. "What better way to get exposure for Ravenswood than for Johnny Conrad himself to stay there?" She smiled.

"Whoa, Ravenswood Manor." Johnny beamed. "*Now* you're talking!"

Adriane smiled at Kara, then stuck her tongue out.

Kara felt unsteady. *What did Adriane think she was doing?* She gestured to Emily. "Do something," she mouthed. Emily shook her head. What could she do? Tell Johnny no?

Kara saw flashes of light and heard the photographers snapping away — and felt the white-hot fire of fury rise within her.

"Outstanding!" Johnny said. "I'd be honored to

make Ravenswood Manor my home away from home." He turned to his entourage. "How do you guys like that for hospitality?"

The members of Johnny's band all nodded enthusiastically.

The crowd cheered.

Adriane strutted past Kara, whispering, "And you thought I wasn't taking any interest in the concert."

It was all Kara could do to keep from screaming at the tall girl.

"I can't wait to practice with Johnny," Adriane said snidely.

"Listen up! I'm going to win that contest," Kara hissed. "It'll be *me* onstage singing with Johnny."

"I guess we'll see about that." Adriane strutted off.

Kara looked around nervously, putting her best smile on display for the crowd as she and her dad prepared to take the activities inside, where the Town Council members and their friends and families would get a chance to meet and greet the great Johnny Conrad.

Ooooh! That Adriane! *I will win,* Kara thought.

There was just one slight glitch: Kara couldn't sing a note in tune if her life depended on it. And everyone knew it.

Chapter 4

Streaks of lavender stretched across the horizon as stars winked into existence. Kara and Emily raced down the gravel driveway to Ravenswood Manor. The girls had about an *hour* before Johnny and his entourage showed up at the manor.

"How could she *do* that?" Kara was steaming at Adriane's totally irritating behavior. "She's trying to outdo me, steal my thunder."

"You're not in this alone, Kara," Emily reminded her.

"Then how are *we* going to get the entire Ravenswood Manor ready?"

"It'll be fine," Emily assured her. "We just have to keep everyone out of the library."

She stopped at the head of the circular driveway. "And we have to keep the magical animals out of sight!"

"About time!" Ozzie called out.

A small gathering of animals milled around in

front of the manor's doors led by Ozzie, Lyra, the pegasus called Balthazar, and Ronif, leader of the ducklike quiffles — all key members of the girls' inner circle of trusted magical animal friends.

"What's kept you?" Ozzie asked, crossing his furry, ferret arms and tapping a rear paw. *"Everyone's waiting for Fairimental updates."*

"Adriane returned a short time ago, acting very strangely," Lyra said softly.

"Strange like how?" Kara asked.

"There have been bursts of her magic all through the manor house."

Kara and Emily exchanged worried glances.

"Looks like we're going to have some guests for a few days," Emily announced to the animals.

"Who?" Balthazar asked.

"Johnny Conrad," Kara said excitedly.

The animals looked at one another, bewildered. Ronif shrugged.

"A musical band," Emily explained.

"I see . . ." Balthazar said worriedly.

"Believe me, I won't forget what Lorelei taught us," Emily said.

The unicorn had shown the girls just how powerful music could be — it created magic, good and bad.

"Gather everyone together back at the glade," Emily ordered. "I want a complete head count."

Ozzie led the animals off toward the lawn behind the manor and the woods beyond.

Kara added, "And make sure everyone stays there!"

"I'm going to assign Storm, Lyra, Balthazar, and Ronif perimeter watch," Emily said. "You find Adriane and see what's going on. And play nice."

"I *can* sing, you know." Kara sniffed.

"Adriane is really talented, too," Emily said. "It's not about who's the best."

"Yeah, it's about being onstage in front of a zillion people with Johnny Conrad!" Kara exclaimed, then added under her breath, "Besides, she started it."

"It doesn't matter who started it. What's important is that the two of you work this out."

Kara frowned. "Okay. But hurry and get back and help me get this place ready. There's probably a million things to do."

Emily dashed off toward the woods following after the animals, while Kara hauled the front door open and bolted into the shadowed foyer of the manor.

"This place is always so dusty and —"

She hit the hall light switch and stopped dead in her tracks.

The manor had been transformed. WELCOME JOHNNY banners and band posters were everywhere, and the manor itself sparkled. Little signs with arrows and notes like THIS WAY TO THE KITCHEN, THIS WAY TO JOHNNY'S ROOM, THIS WAY TO BAND QUARTERS, THIS WAY TO REHEARSAL AREA, and many more were all over the place.

"*Adriane!*" Kara screamed, stomping into the wide lobby.

A loud power chord ripped through the empty halls and echoed throughout the manor. With the volume turned up a notch, a succession of new chords barreled over Kara, bouncing around the entryway in a catchy rhythm.

Adriane was practicing her guitar already? How had she gotten the manor ready so fast? Putting all of this together must have taken days! Unless, of course, she had a little magical help. And Adriane was certainly the most adept at using her magic to make things happen.

Ignoring her relief that everything seemed ready for Johnny, Kara stomped up the wide main staircase to the second floor.

Funky chords shuffled down the hallway as Kara checked through the place. Every room she looked in had been thoroughly cleaned and dusted, sparkling and ready for guests.

Squealing guitar feedback echoed away into silence as Kara walked along the brightly lit corridor to the library. Then she heard something else and froze. Footsteps. From one of the rooms just ahead of her. Someone moving things around.

The lights suddenly went out, closing the hall in darkness. Pale moonlight streamed through a small window at the end of the corridor as Kara's eyes took a moment to adjust. Suddenly, a figure sprang from the library and raced toward the window, cutting a hard left and disappearing down another corridor before Kara could get a decent glimpse of whoever it was.

"Hey, Miss Rock Star!" Kara called out.

She ran toward the window, nearly tripping on a section of rug that had been bunched up. By the time she reached the corridor's intersection, the long hallway leading down to other rooms was empty.

"Adriane, come on!" Kara yelled. She didn't have time for this. Then she noticed a weird, golden glow at her feet, making her shadow stretch far and wide before her. Turning, she saw a flickering light reaching out from the open door to the library.

"Adriane?" she called out, peering inside the library cautiously.

No one was there. The library felt oppressively silent.

Kara walked into the large circular room. Row upon row of books lined the walls. The panel concealing the giant computer screen was closed and untouched. Everything seemed okay.

A shadow moved near Kara's feet. She looked up and stared at the giant mobile that hung from the center of the library's domed ceiling. It was made of a series of celestial pieces, a sun, planets with moons, comets, and stars all designed to swing in synchronous movement. It swayed lightly in the air. Had someone just hurried by it?

Moving under the mobile, she bumped into the large reading table. Rich leather-bound books with gold trim were piled high. Had Adriane been reading all these volumes?

Kara stopped. One of the old musty books lay open. A tall candle cast a wavering light upon its pages. A low, whistling breeze taunted the flame as it flowed into the room from an open window a dozen feet away.

Someone had been in here, reading this book. She looked at the ancient gold lettering along the book's spine, *The Art of Spellsinging.* What kind of research was Adriane doing?

A shuffling noise from out in the hall made Kara spin around again. She didn't like this game Adriane seemed to be playing one bit.

But *was* it Adriane?

She thought about calling Lyra, but Johnny and his people would be there any minute. She examined the book. She was about to close it when the wind kicked up, making the candlelight shine brightly upon one particular passage.

The strongest of magic is the gift of song
In the heart of the spellsinger is where it belongs
Song of truth, words of age
Spread in song what you read on this page
Music will awaken the true power of the
*   lightbringer*
For stars to shine, call upon the spellsinger

Kara stared at the passage for several long moments, the rest of the world, all her responsibilities, even her fight with Adriane, suddenly swept away and forgotten.

The power of the lightbringer? It almost sounded like the book was talking about *her*. She was the blazing star, after all. That's what the Fairimentals said, even if none of the girls had figured out exactly what that meant. The three had been chosen to become mages, magic masters. Emily was to become a healing mage, using the power of her rainbow jewel to help animals. Adriane was a warrior, using the magic of her wolf stone to defend the magic. But Kara hadn't yet found her power. . . . What's a spellsinger? Isn't that what the Fairimental said? Could this be her path?

"What's that you're reading?" a familiar voice said over her shoulder.

Kara jumped and stumbled away from the table, knocking over the candle in the process. She reached for it — but Adriane was closer, and quicker, and snatched the candle before it could fall and harm the book. The dark-eyed girl set it back upright, its flame never going out.

She didn't even look at Kara. She swung her cherry-red electric guitar across her back on its black leather strap and stared at the open pages, her lips forming the words Kara had just read. "Spellsinging. That's cool. . . ."

"Yeah, well, it's better than loud obnoxious power chords! That's like so last century!"

Kara stared daggers at Adriane, but Adriane was oblivious.

"Didn't the Fairimental say something about spellsinging? Where did you find this book?"

Kara crossed her arms. "Oh, like you weren't so reading it before I got here!"

Adriane looked up. "I've never seen it before."

"Tell me another one." Kara paced back and forth under the mobile. "I can't believe you are so jealous that I'm going to sing with Johnny."

"No one said it's going to be you, Miss Center of the Universe," Adriane retorted. "Besides, I wouldn't exactly call what you do singing."

Kara flushed. A loud *squawk* buzzed from her backpack. She fished out the walkie-talkie.

"What!" she snapped.

"Drone One to Queen —"

"Yeah, yeah, what is it?"

"Target on route to Ravenswood —"

Kara's eyes went wide as she shut off the walkie-talkie. "He's coming!" She surveyed the room frantically. There were several strange-looking objects strewn across the tables. "We have to put away anything that looks magical!"

"We can hide everything behind the computer screen," Adriane said, gathering up the books from the table and walking to the secret wall panel. "Since only our jewels can open it, everything should be safe there."

Kara tapped her foot and crossed her arms.

"Oh." Adriane smiled wryly. "I forgot. You don't have a jewel."

"Yet." Kara stepped aside as Adriane lifted her wrist, exposing the amber wolf stone. She held it in front of the secret panel and concentrated. The stone pulsed with golden light outlining the wall with bright lines. The panel silently slid back, revealing the computer screen of the Ravenswood library.

Frustrated, Kara stormed across the room and started gathering items. A snow globe that was anything but what it looked like, several talismans of protection given by the wondrous creatures who had taken refuge in Ravenswood, and a small woven dreamcatcher.

"What's the deal with all these candles?" Adriane asked. "Why didn't you just turn on a light?"

"I thought that was *your* touch. You have been, like, so busy around here," Kara retorted.

"Yeah," Adriane chuckled. "I was cleaning up the manor with Storm, but we weren't in the library —" She looked at Kara, then pointed to the books. "If you didn't find these books and I didn't —"

Kara felt a chill that had nothing to do with the cool air filtering in through the open window. Someone else *had* been here. The person she had glimpsed in the hall hadn't been Adriane. Was that person still here, in the manor?

She regarded the open window. "Someone else has been here," Kara said stiffly.

"No way," Adriane disagreed, picking up the book about spellsinging again. "Storm would have warned me if someone had snuck into the manor."

Kara dumped the items she had gathered behind the secret panel.

"I think I'll hold on to this," Adriane said, opening the book again. "I understand music better than you, anyway. If there's something important here about musical magic, I should know about it." She gave Kara a quick glance. "And this could be very useful for my singing debut with Johnny."

Kara's entire body tensed. She was about to start screaming when something sparkled from the hiding place. Kara's eyes opened wide. It was the horn of the unicorn Lorelei, given to Emily to lead the girls across the magic web and back home to Ravenswood. The power of the horn was supposed to grant the user *any* magic he or she desired. Kara cut a quick glimpse back at Adriane and saw that the raven-haired girl was riffling through the pages.

With one quick, furtive motion, Kara snatched the crystalline unicorn horn and slipped it in her backpack.

Emily was right, Kara decided. It didn't matter who started this business between her and Adriane — only who finished it.

In other words, whoever stood onstage with Johnny Conrad, singing in front of the world, the envy of everyone, was the winner!

The unicorn horn sparkled with magical energy as she closed her backpack.

Chapter 5

Kara heard the knock at the manor's front door and only barely beat Adriane to it. She smiled brightly as Johnny and his manager, a dude called Inky Toon, stepped inside.

Johnny was, as always, totally laid-back and cool.

"Hello, paradise!" Johnny whistled as he looked around the spacious foyer. "This place is awesome!"

"Cool crib, girl," Inky said. "You know what I say, life is always a par-tay, and this is a place where we can work it."

Kara smiled. "Welcome to Ravenswood Manor. I'll be happy to show you guys the digs."

Looking vexed that Kara was getting credit for welcoming Johnny and his people to the manor, Adriane cleared her throat. Inky nodded toward the raven-haired girl and handed her his leather jacket. "Yo, guitar girl — hang that up for me? We got a few things out in the car, too. Thanks!"

Adriane took the jacket, adjusting the guitar still hung over her back, and walked off with it. "Yeah, sure, you're welcome. . . ."

"A few more are arriving shortly," Inky said.

"A few more?" Kara stopped in mid-grin.

"Yeah, you know what I'm sayin — we got our crew to take care of."

"Sure . . . okay, I guess."

Soon, the entire mansion was buzzing. Johnny's band and all his technical people had arrived, along with Emily and Gran. Adriane's grandmother looked concerned about the way the manor was being taken over. Gran even took Adriane outside for what looked like a stern talking-to.

Good, Kara thought.

The band's equipment took over the immense dining room, which would be used for rehearsal space. The parlor, kitchen, and adjoining sitting rooms were overflowing with the newcomers. Kara found Emily and led her to the main living room to "mix it up!" as Kara had put it.

Someone slipped a disk in a boom box and the room filled with a hip-hop blaster that was tearing up the charts. Johnny spun around the room demonstrating some of the hot dance moves that had catapulted him to stardom. Everyone cheered and got into the groove.

Kara leaned next to Emily against the wall beside the fireplace. Johnny had a way of making her feel so relaxed. He was just *so* cool.

"What do you think of Johnny?" she asked.

Emily fluttered her hand over her heart and rolled her eyes. "He is so cute!"

"Back at ya!"

"Everything okay with you and Adriane?" Emily asked.

Kara tensed, suddenly thinking of the unicorn horn she had swiped. Guilt overwhelmed her at the thought of Emily finding out what she had done. "Don't ask."

"That bad?"

"Worse." Kara remembered the book she'd found in the library — and the mysterious visitor who must have been looking it over. She told Emily about it and they quietly slipped upstairs to investigate further, away from their company. They unlocked the library and went inside. Emily popped on the light. She started — and pointed at the rug. "Look!"

Kara focused on the large woven area rug by the door. The red, blue, and gold weave was splotched with brown.

"Someone tracked mud in here," Emily said. Those weren't splotches — they were footprints. Looking closer, she determined the prints were wide, with three toes. "Only these prints are not human. Some kind of animal."

Kara and Emily exchanged worried glances. "It can't be bad," Kara remarked, remembering what Adriane had told her. "Storm would have warned us."

"That Fairimental told you to be careful," Emily reminded her.

Was this what the Fairimental had meant? Maybe this "spellsinging" stuff had something to do with helping them.

"Is that the book?" Emily asked.

"That's it." Kara had seen Adriane put the book into her backpack, then rush out without it when the doorbell rang. Smugly, she had retrieved it.

For an instant, Kara thought she heard someone humming or singing in the hall. Then the sound faded.

Deciding it was just music from downstairs, Emily and Kara read a passage from the book:

Spellsing as one
And see your work done
Spellsing as three
And whatever you picture will be

"It sounds like it's talking about us," Emily said. "The power of three."

49

"But what's spellsinging?"

"Some kind of spell-casting using music?" Emily suggested.

"You think whatever was in here was looking for this magic?"

"Knock, knock," a deep voice called.

"Ahhh!" the girls cried together.

Kara and Emily spun to see Johnny standing in the open doorway, leaning against the frame with his confident grin. Kara thought she had closed and locked the door behind them. Apparently, she'd been too distracted.

"What an incredible room!" Johnny eased into the library, looking around and admiring all the shelves of books and the odd little curios, all fashioned in an animal motif. "So this is the famous Ravenswood Manor library!"

Kara slapped the book closed and passed it to Emily, who slid it behind her back.

"Look at all these books!" he continued, walking around the circular room. "And these paintings are awesome! An original Parrish, a Bates, and this . . . whoa! The Munro Orrery." He gazed up at the intricate mobile.

"Awesome," Kara agreed, totally in awe of her guest.

"How do you know so much about Ravenswood?" Emily asked.

"I'm a history-head." Johnny smiled. "Especially when it comes to haunted houses."

"Haunted houses?" Emily glanced at Kara.

"Yeah, I live for this stuff. Ravenswood and the woods around the preserve are famous, full of ghosts, witches, and monsters!" He laughed.

"The woods aren't haunted," Emily said. "That's just kids' stories."

"No? I'm sure there are some extra-special things going on here." Johnny's deep blue eyes sparkled as he smiled.

Kara nudged Emily's arm. "Maybe you should take our *homework* to Adriane."

"Yeah, good idea," Emily said, bumping into bookshelves as she edged out the door.

"Soooo," Kara said, smiling and sidling to the reading table, away from the secret computer panel. "You're a Ravenswood buff. That's cool, Johnny." Her smile faltered and her heart started racing and suddenly she felt like a complete buffoon. "Johnny. I called you Johnny. . . . *Can* I call you Johnny? Or should it be Mr. Conrad, or Mr. C, or —"

Johnny laughed, and it was such a friendly laugh, an almost musical sound, that it instantly calmed Kara's sudden case of the jitters.

"Johnny's my name, don't wear it out." The rock star smiled, turning his baby blues to the rows of books. "I love to read." He ran long fingers over the rich leather-bound volumes.

"You do?"

He laughed again and a warm, comforting breeze seemed to caress her.

"Of course," Johnny said softly as he intently scanned the titles on the shelves. "I'm on the road all the time. I've got to do something to make it less boring."

"Boring?" Kara asked incredulously. "Your life, boring? I don't believe it."

He glanced her way. "Well, there are some pretty exciting moments. Like meeting new people and seeing new places. . . ."

His sigh even sounded like music, and it made Kara's heart beat like thunder.

"And getting up onstage," Johnny said quickly, "performing for my fans, singing my music. It's like . . . magic." He turned to face Kara, and for a split second, she caught a flash of fire in his eyes.

Kara took a step back. She felt feverish. This was unreal. *She* was spending time alone with Johnny Conrad!

Just wait until she told Heather and Molly about this. . . .

"So you're a singer, too," Johnny said brightly.

Kara was startled. "Huh?"

"Your dad told me you were dying to win the

contest. You and your pal with the guitar. Though I hope for her sake that she's got one top-notch voice, 'cause you've got her way beat where it counts."

Kara nearly choked. "I do? R — r — really?"

"I know about these things," he said, low, musical tones seeming to echo beneath each of his words . . . words that filled her with that same confidence that radiated from the singer. "You've got something special. I can feel it. You know what that is?"

Kara thought of the unicorn horn. . . . No, that was crazy. Johnny didn't have anything to do with magic. He was talking about something inside her, a special quality.

"Star power," he answered for her. "And I'm never wrong."

Before Kara could even think of what to say in reply, Inky and two others were in the doorway.

"Wow. What a spread!" Inky commented, taking in the vast library. "This place rocks!"

"Come on, Johnny, press is here," one of the others said, nodding her gold-and-pink-haired head into the room. "We promised you'd do some interviews."

"Okay," Johnny said, walking to the door. He turned back and gave Kara a wink. "Star power," he repeated.

Johnny left Kara and went into the hallway. As she heard them hurry off, she felt her head start to clear and realized she'd have to be more careful in the future. This library had to remain off-limits to visitors. And there was the computer, which held secret knowledge about subjects practically beyond imagining, like other worlds.

She locked the door on her way out.

Star power! Kara beamed. "Finally, someone notices!"

❧　❧　❧

Late that night, an exhausted Emily dropped onto her bed without even bothering to change into pajamas. She wanted to read more of the book she had taken from the mansion. . . . What little she had read about spellsinging had completely captured her imagination. Magic spellcasting with music — awesome!

What a day this had been — and things were only going to get more exciting. It would all be wonderful, absolutely perfect — if only Kara and Adriane could work out their differences.

Then again, there was that warning from the Fairimental. Was something going on? Had the Dark Sorceress set another of her plots in motion to take advantage of how busy and distracted the girls were now that Johnny was at Ravenswood? Emily decided tomorrow they would have to get

Kara to call the dragonflies. They would contact Zach, on Aldenmor, and find out what was happening there. Whatever the Dark Sorceress was up to, it was not good.

Clank!

Slam!

Cheep-cheep!

Emily bolted upright in bed, still fully dressed. Those sounds had come from outside. She ran to the window and looked out at the converted barn behind their house.

"Eeep-eep-ooooook!"

"Krrrrang!"

Someone was in the Pet Palace.

Emily burst from her bedroom, zoomed downstairs, and headed toward the back door.

"Emily?" her mom called out. Carolyn had been downstairs in her office with a reporter, a journalist who wanted an animal specialist's viewpoint on the Ravenswood Preserve.

"Just checking on Dr. Ehrlich's monkeys," Emily called out as she whizzed by.

She ran across the small expanse of yard and entered the Pet Palace. Bizarre! Some old woman was prying open the cages that held the former circus monkeys and letting them go free!

"Hey!" Emily hollered.

The old woman turned and Emily froze. Fear

ripped up her spine, tickling the hairs on her neck. Mrs. Windor's eyes glowed with red fire. She was hunched over, slobbering like a wild animal. A long tongue wagged from her mouth as saliva dripped to the wooden floor. A sudden burst of white light filled the space. For a moment, Emily didn't know what had happened — then she saw her mother appear outside the nearby open window and saw the reporter with a flash camera.

Dr. Carolyn Fletcher's jaw dropped. "What's going on in here? What are you —"

The photographer snapped another shot, his flash blinding mother and daughter.

"Yiieeeee-eeek-eeek-eeek!"

The monkeys howled and hollered, the sudden flash making them leap from the top of one cage to another.

"Sorry," the photographer said. Screaming madly, Mrs. Windor flung herself past the astonished group and out the door, running across the backyard, toward the woods. The monkeys followed, one flying through the window and knocking the photographer flat on his back before bounding off into the darkness, another racing around and leading Emily and her mother in circles before running off and escaping through the open back door.

In the distance, Mrs. Windor cackled like a wild beast.

Emily and her mother went outside, just in time to see the photographer drive off in his car.

"What was *that* all about?" Emily's mom asked, startled.

Emily knew Mrs. Windor wanted to disrupt the concert any way she could and prove to everyone the animals here weren't safe. But this was crazy! And the way Mrs. Windor had looked. Almost as if she weren't human. A cold chill lodged in her spine.

Shaking her head, Emily said, "I guess Mrs. Windor finally went over the edge."

They went back inside to grab flashlights so they could hunt for the missing monkeys.

Had they remained outside, they might have seen Mrs. Windor peeking out from behind the tallest tree at the edge of the grove, watching their house carefully . . . and they might have heard the strange little song she hummed.

The monkeys came to her then, their heads lolling, their eyes glazed, looking completely entranced by the sounds she made.

Then, suddenly, Mrs. Windor bent low and hissed at the animals, her features melting and changing, her skin turning green and scaly, her eyes turning to smoldering yellow slits in the night, her teeth sharpening to nasty little points.

The monkeys shrieked and ran off in terror as the creature who used to be Beasley Windor straightened to its full seven-foot form, its long arms swaying, its claws clicking and clacking in the near dark. It leaned back its massive head and roared.

Across the expanse of woods, deep in the heart of Ravenswood, cries of fear erupted in the magic glade. Magical animals that had been sleeping soundly suddenly awoke, horrified by the presence they sensed, a monstrous apparition: a creature dank and foul, from the darkest depths of their worst nightmares. And it was here.

Chapter 6

The morning sun cast deep, long shadows behind Kara as she trudged along the high, grassy bank of the Chitakaway River, head down, feet dragging. She swung her backpack by its straps, letting it graze the dewy grass and earth, not even caring if it collected stains. Sparkling water danced and crashed over wide, flat stones jutting from the river, the roaring and rushing creating its own special music.

She had suffered the most restless night's sleep she could possibly have imagined, one minute flying high in amazing dreams of success, basking in the glow of superstardom, the envy of all her friends — and the next, tossed into throes of anxiety, running scared in the blackest nightmares of failure, feeling utter humiliation as everyone laughed at her, their hoots and snickers echoing in her mind.

"Okay, okay, just breathe," Kara said aloud, painfully aware of her own shortcomings as a singer — and the event looming over her this evening: The preliminary karaoke-style audition for the big contest would be held at seven in the main auditorium. Inky Toon would pick five lucky winners who'd be allowed to sing during the preshow on Saturday. Johnny would judge that round of competition personally.

Kara would have to sing in front of dozens of people tonight — maybe even hundreds . . . including Adriane.

She clutched her backpack tighter, tormented by indecision. She could feel the unicorn horn inside, radiating with power, calling to her. Yet she also felt a nagging twinge of guilt for taking it in the first place, and for what she planned on doing with it. She knew the effect she had upon Emily's and Adriane's jewels, amplifying their power, allowing them to do amazing things with their magic. Why should she, Kara Davies, have to play the role of helper, powering their magic as they honed and fine-tuned *their* skills? What if she had no special magic of her own or worse, was destined to *never* have a stone?

No! She had felt the call of the magic before. A shiver passed through her. She was chosen, too, you know. With trembling fingers, Kara opened the backpack and touched the unicorn horn. It felt cool and solid in her hand.

She remembered the wild magic of the unicorn

jewel she had found a month ago. In her hands, that jewel was awesome in its power. Although she had given it back to the unicorn's maidens, the magic of the unicorn jewel had awakened in her feelings that would never again lie dormant. Feelings that would not, could not, be denied. A part of her needed to unleash the magic. It lay pent up inside, dark, cold, and vicious, like a coiled snake, ready to strike.

A fluttering in the breeze behind her made her turn just in time to see Lyra descend. Kara marveled at the cat's powerful magic wings. Unlike the feathery butterfly-shaped wings of a pegasus, Lyra's were sleek, hawklike, built for speed and fast maneuvering. The tapered, golden wings folded to the cat's sides, flashed, and disappeared.

"No ride this morning?" Lyra asked, brushing up against Kara's hip.

Kara scratched the great cat behind the ears and shrugged. "I decided to walk."

"Storm and I checked the entire preserve. We've found no sign of any intruder that scared the animals last night."

"Maybe it was just a nightmare," Kara said.

"Then they all had the same nightmare."

"Even if something bad had managed to slip through the dreamcatcher, you or Storm would have sensed anything dangerous."

"Just the same, with all these fans starting to arrive in Ravenswood, we're on high alert."

"Okay." Kara looked down, shuffling her feet.

"Are you still concerned about this singing contest?"

"No! Yes. Maybe . . ."

"You sounded great the other morning."

"Yeah, it's easy when you have a band like Be*Tween to sing along with. Tonight I have to sing all by myself!"

"You're making too much out of this." Lyra whammed her flank playfully against Kara, hard enough to make the girl wobble for a second before regaining her footing.

"Quit it! I am not! The entire school is going to be there!"

As they neared the Saddleback Bridge that would take Kara over the river and onto the main road to the middle school, Lyra stopped and sat back on her haunches.

"Okay, let's hear," Lyra said.

"What, now?" Kara stopped, irritated.

"Give it your best shot," the cat said patiently.

Kara looked around. A few blackbirds sat in an ancient oak. Other than the birds, the area was empty.

She took a breath. "Okay, you asked for it." She put down her backpack and struck her best singing-star pose.

She hummed a bit and started her choreographed steps, adding a few new ones she picked up watching Johnny and his crew.

Lyra bobbed her head along. *"Good moves, but can you sing a little louder?*

Kara went for it.

> *I've got it made*
> *I know someone really loves me*
> *Someone who won't turn me away*
> *I'm not afraid*
> *With the strength of us together*
> *Nothing's going to stand in our way*

The blackbirds screamed in protest of the obnoxious, screeching voice that had interrupted their day. They flew away, squawking back a few insults.

Lyra listened patiently. Kara couldn't tell if the cat was smiling or about to hurl a furball.

> *I know with time*
> *We'll get closer every minute*
> *Know each other's secrets so well*
> *We'll touch the sky and we'll find a new tomorrow*
> *We'll discover dreams in ourselves*
> *After all we've been through*
> *I know I've found a friend in you*

Kara swung around and faced Lyra. "Well?"

Lyra sat for a second then stretched her back and stood. *"Well . . ."*

"I knew it." Kara swept up her backpack and stomped off. "I stink!"

Lyra caught up to her. *"I wouldn't say that."*

"Well, what would you say?"

"You just need a little help."

"Exactly what I was thinking!" Kara looked relieved as she held up her backpack.

"A few lessons with a singing coach and maybe choir practice."

"Oh — yeah . . ." Kara lowered the backpack.

Lyra cocked her head. *"What were you thinking?"*

"Uh . . . yeah, I should practice with the choir," she said, embarrassed now to admit what she was *really* thinking about.

They headed across the pedestrian bridge. Beyond it lay the road leading to the school. Kara knew that Lyra would have to turn back once they got there, or else risk drawing attention. That meant if Kara wanted to tell Lyra what was on her mind, she'd have to do it quickly. Yet she was torn.

As much as Kara deeply needed to unburden herself to her friend, there were so many things she was trying to come to grips with. She wasn't exactly proud of what she had done, and though she knew she could trust Lyra, Kara still worried about how the cat would react once she knew the truth — not only had she taken the unicorn horn after the girls had made a promise to one another to always keep it hidden away, but she was planning to use the magic for her own selfish gain.

"Lyra, have you ever done something you know you really shouldn't have? Something a part of you wishes you could take back, while another part of you is saying, hey, I'd do it again."

The cat's eyes twinkled. *"Why are you asking?"*

Kara looked away. If she told the cat about the unicorn horn, she'd never be able to keep it; she'd feel too guilty about making Lyra an accomplice after the fact.

"This thing you're talking about," Lyra said, *"it can't be undone?"*

The thought finally occurred to Kara that she could go to the manor *right now* and put the unicorn horn where it belonged. Provided she wasn't caught, no one would ever know she'd taken it in the first place.

But . . . she needed it. How could she hope to compete in the contest *without* using magic? Magic that was given to the girls. Well, to Emily actually. But it had been given to help all three of them.

"She's your friend, she will understand," Lyra said. *"I think you should just talk to her."*

"Huh?" Kara asked, startled.

"Adriane's just stubborn, unlike someone else I know," the cat said, rubbing playfully against Kara's side.

"Yeah," Kara said, quickly recovering from her surprise. "She should be apologizing to me!"

Lyra sighed.

"I've got to get to school!" Kara rushed ahead, anxious to get away from Lyra before she was forced to look her friend in the eye — she knew she couldn't do that — and tell a lie, even a little white lie like pretending she'd meant Adriane all along.

❦ ❦ ❦

Kara lasted exactly three class periods before the urge to do something she had never done before became overpowering. She couldn't concentrate on classwork. She only barely heard Emily as the girl went on about the craziness with Mrs. Windor the night before, which, thanks to the picture-snapping reporter, was even more fully reported in the morning edition of the *Stonehill Gazette*.

Kara barely paid attention even as Heather, Molly, and Tiffany crowded around her, wanting to know all the details of what Johnny Conrad was really like. She was the "center of the universe," as Adriane had put it, just like she wanted to be . . . but for how long?

Just before fourth period, she did something she'd never done before — Kara cut class.

Soon she was outside the building, standing behind a large maple tree. Peering around the tree, she saw the open doors that led from the music room to the track behind the school. The ground was worn in spots from the treads of large tires. Vans and trucks were often parked here so that big pieces of musical equipment could be moved in and out for sporting events or performances around town.

She listened to the uplifting voices of the school's choir practicing in the spacious music room. They sounded so rich and beautiful. A soloist took the lead and Kara sang along, desperately attempting to match the girl's incredible voice. But every note Kara sang was either flat or sharp, early or late, always somehow just plain wrong. Even when she tried to take the easier route of singing along with the rest of the choir, she was never in tune with them.

Kara tried to belt it out like she did when singing along to Be*Tween. A few stray dogs ran around the tree, barking. She quickly shut her mouth, looking around. The last thing she needed was to get caught and end up in detention. As it was, she kept an eye on the time. She had a route figured out that would get her back inside and to the nurse's station way before the period was over. She even had her lines scripted in advance: *Oh, Nurse Sherman, I felt so faint. I have so much going on with the benefit concert and everything. . . .*

And the nurse would say Kara was pushing herself too hard — which was true — and write her an excuse to give to her fourth-period teacher so she wouldn't get in trouble for cutting.

She had it all worked out — the only problem was that this little practice session wasn't helping. For a moment, she thought about just giving up. Then she thought of Adriane's defiant, triumphant smile, the one she'd give her when Kara wimped out.

No, she *had* to sing at the contest tonight. She had to make it to the final round and prove to Adriane that she was . . . that she was *someone. The best!*

Johnny thought she was. He said she had something special: star power.

And he should know.

Okay, Kara knew that in this arena, she was no match for Adriane. Not without a lot of practice — or a little magical help. Adriane had used magic to get Ravenswood all ready for Johnny. Why shouldn't Kara use magic now?

She opened her backpack and took out the unicorn horn. The crystalline horn shone in the noon sun, rainbow sparkles running up and down its intricately spiraled curves.

"I want to sing like a star!" Kara said.

She held it tight and tried a chorus of "Supernatural High."

It wasn't working — she sounded just the same. Kara felt close to panicking. This was her last hope. What's she doing wrong? Maybe the horn worked just for Emily.

I need to focus, like Emily and Adriane do when they use their stones, she thought.

Think musical magic. Magic to make music. Music to make magic. She thought of the book she had found in the library. The strange words of spellsinging drifted in her mind.

Spellsing as one
And see your work done

"Okay . . ." Kara whispered. Spellsinging. What did that have to do with seeing her "work done"?

A good spell could help focus energy.

I want to sing like a bird
The best in the world
Make my voice ring
I'm super-stylin'

Cute, she thought. Not too bad for her first magic spell.

She tried saying the words again, but nothing happened. Then she tried singing them in a rapping rhythm, the unicorn horn clutched tightly in her hand. Suddenly, she felt the wind kick up around her, lifting her long blond hair.

Whoa!

It stopped the moment she fell silent.

Kara tried the spell again, singing the words a little more loudly now, with more confidence and control — and somehow, even though she wasn't singing what the choir was singing, she was in tune with them, her rhythms in sync, her notes flowing perfectly with theirs.

An ember of brilliant blue light suddenly flared from the horn. Kara leaped back, scared. She watched in amazement as the light spread between her fingers. Kara felt dizzy as power grew in her hands, a massive force building. The air felt heavy as it swirled around her. Her heart thundered in a chorus of power.

This was wrong! She knew it and fought against its call. But another part of her sang with the harmonies of her magic. *Her magic!* The power was exhilarating. The wind screamed in her ears, whipping around her in a mad cyclone of magically charged air.

Her hands blazed with blue fire as the magic crackled across her skin. The power seemed so much larger than her small frame. How could it stay contained? And once released, how could she control it?

Taking a deep breath, she cleared her mind of anything but the flows and ebbs of the magic. In a few heartbeats, the glow grew back to an intense blaze. She could do this!

Kara squeezed her eyes closed and centered her breathing. With a certainty that rocked her world, she locked the magic to her will.

Kara started to sing. A perfect "A" note rang from her mouth. She moved to a C, an F-sharp, then began running up the scale, notes perfectly in tune, each rising in perfect pitch. Her control was incredible. Her voice became a lilting, wondrous sound, cascading like sweet summer rain as it moved up and down the scale.

The horn blazed with power. The magic inside of her sang for release.

And Kara was ready.

She raced up a three-octave scale and, with perfect breath control, she hit a triple high C.

Magic exploded from the horn, a cold fire raging out into the world.

The tree trunk burst with an explosive *crack*!

Waves of invisible force rippled out from her

body, her mind, her soul — as a window shattered in the school!

She heard the choir screaming in surprise.

A flicker of a smile fluttered around her mouth before Kara forced her lips to a stern line — but somewhere deep inside, somewhere she feared to look too closely, a part of her crackled with wicked delight. The magic was hers.

     ❧   ❧   ❧

"You can go now, Mrs. Windor," the desk sergeant said as he opened the cell door.

"It's about time!" Mrs. Windor clutched a copy of the *Stonehill Gazette,* revealing the photograph of her at the Pet Palace, a monkey on her back. "I was nowhere near that house!"

The sergeant looked at her wearily. He was a big man with salt-and-pepper hair. "Uh-huh. Besides the pictures, there were three eyewitness accounts. The photographer, Dr. Fletcher, her daughter . . ."

"All of them at Ravenswood are in on this together. I bet it was that Mrs. Chardáy who dressed up as me for these clearly *staged* photographs!"

"Ah," the officer said. "And why would she do that?"

"To discredit me, of course."

The desk sergeant said, "I'm just stating the facts, ma'am. Now why don't you go home, cool off, and have a nice long rest? You might even consider seeing a . . . doctor."

"That was not me last night!" Mrs. Windor shrieked as she nervously backed out of the building.

The desk sergeant was no longer listening. Instead, he was watching out of the corner of his eye to see if the door might be kind enough to hit Mrs. Windor in the rear end on her way out.

"Whaaaah!" she yelped.

He chuckled as it did.

Chapter 7

The chaos caused by Kara's accidental magical window shattering turned to an advantage when she reached the nurse's office. No one had been hurt by the shattered glass. But a lot of students had been badly shaken by the sudden "windstorm." She was checked out and got a note to excuse her for missing fourth period.

The worst of it was that Kara *knew* she should feel terrible about what she had done — but she didn't. She carefully tested her new vocal proficiency as she walked down the hallway. Humming a tune under her breath, she heard a light musical ringing and felt a tingling throughout her body. After what happened outside, she couldn't risk anything louder. She was dying to find out what the effects of the spell involved were, and if they were lasting. As soon as she could get free, she had to find a secluded area to do further tests. She just had to force herself to make it through the rest of the school day.

Her greatest frustration was that she didn't

have the spellsinging book. If she had been more on top of things, she would have gotten it back from Emily the night before. But the time spent with Johnny had cast kind of a spell on her, making her feel light-headed with joy, not able to think as clearly as she usually did. And today, whenever she was with her pals Heather, Molly, and Tiffany, she could hardly concentrate. All she could think about was spellsinging. And Johnny.

Finally, the three o'clock bell sounded, and Kara rushed to her locker. All around her, kids were buzzing with excitement over the karaoke contest to take place this evening. Kara ignored them all, collecting her backpack and her books as fast as she could.

"Hey!"

She looked up to see Adriane standing there, glaring at her.

"Hey is for horses."

"You haven't said one word to me or Emily today, and now you're rushing off again!" Adriane said angrily. The wolf stone on Adriane's wrist suddenly pulsed with hot light as Kara lifted her backpack from her locker. Adriane quickly covered her wrist with the sleeve of her jacket.

Adriane leaned in close and hissed, "Aren't you even the least bit concerned about what happened to the animals last night?"

"No. Should I be?"

"They think some kind of monster might have gotten through the dreamcatcher," Adriane whispered, glancing around to make sure no one else was listening.

"A monster *can't* get through. That's the whole point, duh!"

"We need you to make a dragonfly call to Zach."

Kara bit her lip. This was so not the time for those pests!

"And just where were you when that 'windstorm' hit?" Adriane asked suspiciously, rubbing her gemstone as if it irritated her.

"Uh . . . getting stuff done . . ." Kara held the backpack behind her, as far away from Adriane's wrist as she could.

"You have to get this concert back under control. Gran is getting really annoyed."

"You were the one who put Johnny and his people at Ravenswood. Don't come crying to me!" Kara pointed out.

"This is *your* show, superstar! You need to get over to Ravenswood right now and finalize a million details."

"I can't. . . . I . . . I'm busy."

Adriane's eyebrow raised. "With what?"

"I'm going to . . ." Guilt flashed through her.

There might be something dangerous at the preserve. The girls had no idea what was going on in Aldenmor. They needed to talk to Zach. And there *were* a million details to deal with on the concert.

Kara sighed. All she really wanted to do was lose herself in the dream that was Johnny and her sharing the spotlight, singing before a crowd, basking in their love —

Shouts and screams broke her thoughts. Hundreds of kids were suddenly pouring out the front door of the school.

What now? Kara thought as she followed and bolted from the building.

Suddenly, everyone turned to look at her. Silence fell as the crowd parted like a sea to reveal a long black limo parked by the curb. Johnny stood to the side, leaning on the car's trunk, grinning as the horde of fans flocked around him.

Laughing, he signed notebooks, articles of clothing, even one kid's arm. Then he turned and looked right at Kara.

"Good luck with the contest, everyone. We'll be seeing you all at the show tomorrow." He raised a fist into the air. "Ravenswood!" he shouted.

"Johnny!" the crowd yelled back. "Johnny!"

"Let's hear it for the other star of this concert. The one responsible for the entire show," Johnny said, holding out his hand in Kara's direction. Kara walked through the crowd in a daze. Johnny opened the rear door for Kara to climb in. Then he hopped into the other side, and in seconds, they were off.

Kara was startled at the cheers and cries from behind them, and shocked when she looked back at the expressions on the faces of so many kids; they were calling Kara's name just as often as Johnny's, and many looked at her with the same awe they had reserved for the singer.

From the corner of her eye, she glanced at Adriane yelling something. Ooo, she must be so jealous! Smiling to herself, Kara turned and settled back in her seat, as the limo left the school far behind.

"You know, anyone who tells you it isn't fun being a star is either lying or crazy." Johnny smiled as they drove on, heading toward a scenic road that skirted the woods and fields surrounding Stonehill.

Kara nodded. For a moment, *she* had been the one so many people were looking at with adoration. . . .

"But I'm not a star, I mean like you are," she said self-consciously.

"Don't be so modest," he said. "You put this whole show together. Everyone in this town knows you're special."

That pretty much was true, Kara thought. Not to brag, but the facts spoke for themselves. She'd been the most popular girl in school even before all this stuff with the concert started up.

"The way I figure it, sometimes that light's already there, inside a person," Johnny mused.

"What light?" Kara asked.

"The light that makes someone shine like a star. The only difference between the people who make it and those who don't is whether or not those people are willing to do whatever it takes to make the whole world see that light."

Kara raised her chin and tossed back her golden hair. "I want to make the whole world see what I'm about."

"There you go," Johnny said, his voice once again sounding like music, a perfect, enchanting song that made her feel better about everything, more confident than she had in days. She had done the right thing using the unicorn horn. She knew that now.

Johnny continued, "Everyone does whatever they have to do to get what they want. It's a game. The only thing that matters is if you play to win. There's the easy way and the hard way of handling things. Why take the long road around and have to wait for something you want when someone's pointing out a shortcut?"

Thinking about the karaoke contest, Kara couldn't have agreed more.

Cool as it was listening to him, being with him, Kara had something more urgent to do. She had to practice for the audition! She asked to be dropped off near the orchard fields. She could walk home from there.

Johnny signaled to the driver and the limo stopped by the side of the road.

Kara smiled as she hopped out of the car. "Thanks for the ride."

"Anytime," Johnny said rummaging in a bag. "Wait . . . Here, take this."

Kara took the small locket on a slim gold chain he handed her.

"I was given this before my first big show. It brought me luck." He shrugged. "Now you can use it to bring *you* luck."

Kara nodded eagerly. "Wow. Thanks." She clutched the locket in her hand.

"I thought you might like to have it with you for the first round tonight. Not that I think you'll need it — I know you're gonna knock everyone out." Johnny winked.

You've never even heard me sing, Kara thought, suddenly horrified. Then she relaxed. After all, she had the unicorn horn, plus she was learning about spellsinging, her secret weapon.

Her sudden confidence must have shown on her face, because Johnny winked at her. Then the limo headed off down the country road.

Kara looked at the locket in her hand. She would wear it during the preliminary judging tonight.

She took a deep breath, put the locket in her backpack, and looked around. She was alone. She crossed the field to the pedestrian bridge that arched over the Chitakaway River. The oaks and maples were so thick on both sides, she knew no one would see or hear her practicing. The beautiful suspension bridge arched like a web over the flowing waters that ran in the ravine far below. She set off across, feeling the bridge gently sway under her feet. About halfway across, she stopped and took a breath.

There's magic in the air
Love is everywhere
All our friends are gathered round
To celebrate the fair

Kara was shocked. Her voice screeched across the ravine. Whatever happened before *wasn't* happening now. Her voice hadn't improved! She tried three more times, but her singing didn't get any better. What was she going to do? How would

Johnny react when he heard her voice for the first time and it wasn't as wonderful as he thought it would be?

Johnny wasn't like everyone else. He really listened to her. He respected her point of view, and he was willing to talk to her in ways no one ever had before.

She had no choice now. Opening her backpack, she took out the horn. This time she would be more careful. She felt the energy already sparking in her hands as she held the horn out in front of her. The words of spellsinging raced through her mind

Spellsing as one
And see your work done

The magic of the unicorn was just what she needed to jump-start her spell!

Sing a spell make it come true
Let my voice ring loud and clear
Change how I sing, and what they hear
I'll be as perfect as can be,
Make each note a part of me.

Blue fire flashed in the horn. She was a little nervous as she felt the winds kick up, the bridge tremble lightly as it swayed, then pulse like a backbeat. Soon, her fear melted away into pure anticipation and excitement. Power surged forth from the horn, but this time she was ready, holding it fast with her will.

She opened her mouth and tried again.

The sun goes round the moon
The flowers are in bloom
You got to follow every dream
'Cause your time is coming soon
Feel the magic Can you feel it
Feel the magic Can you feel it

This time, her voice carried true, ringing out across the river in waves of sonic bliss. She sang perfectly in tune, every word as perfect as she had heard it on the Be*Tween CD. Tapping her feet to the rhythm, Kara started to dance on the bridge. Arms moving in a tight routine, she felt light as air, dancing in the orange glow of the afternoon sun.

A dark shadow passed overhead. Kara spun, and the bridge swayed. Still in step, she looked up at wide, fluffy white clouds, rolling under a blue-domed sky. She continued her singing. No one had a chance against her style. She was super-stylin'!

BUMP!

The bridge lunged sideways, throwing Kara off

balance. Something had knocked into it from underneath. Underneath? She was at least ten stories in the air. She held the rope railing as the bridge settled, and peered out. The river ran fast, cascading over the rocks below and sending sprays of water high into the air.

Kara began to get an uneasy feeling in the pit of her stomach as she slipped the unicorn horn into her backpack. She was about to start for the far side of the bridge when the dark shadow passed over her feet. She whipped her head up and squinted against the sun. Something big was flying right toward her. Then she saw the familiar golden wings and spotted fur. She let out her breath.

"Geez, Lyra, you scared me half to death!"

The cat angled down over the far side of the bridge and swooped straight at her, coming in fast.

"What's with you?" Kara slipped her arms into her backpack. She looked up just as Lyra collided into her, sending Kara flying back. The girl was driven to the floor of the bridge, the wind knocked out of her.

"*Lyra!*" she sputtered, shaken to the core. "What are you doing?"

Kara tried to get back on her feet but Lyra was too swift and strong. The cat smashed into her back, and Kara slammed face-first against the railing. She found herself staring straight down at the rushing river below.

Kara was too astonished to even think. Cold fear rushed up her body as she scrambled back onto the bridge. Clutching the rope, she turned — just as the cat roared and lunged for her again. Sharp claws raked down her side, tearing out patches of denim and silk.

"Lyra!" Kara screamed, beating her arms to keep the razor claws from slicing at her neck and face. "Stop it!"

The cat brutally swiped at the girl, sending Kara hurtling toward the other side of the bridge. The rope caught her stomach, almost flipping her completely over. She crumbled to the bridge, her sweater ripped, one long gash down her left leg.

"Please! Lyra, don't hurt me!" she cried out. Sweeping sweat-streaked hair from her face, she tried to scramble across the bridge. Her left leg gave out and she stumbled. Her eyes caught glimpses of the riverbank only a few dozen yards away, and the path to her house that lay beyond it.

Lyra landed on the bridge, blocking Kara's way. The cat crouched, the fur on her flanks upright, her eyes dark with cold fire. Baring razor teeth, snarling low and vicious, the cat advanced.

Tears streaming down her face, Kara searched

her friend's eyes, looking for an answer. "I didn't mean to lie to you."

Lyra stared at Kara as if the girl were a hated enemy — one to be torn from this world.

"I took the horn . . . I'm sorry," she cried. Kara pushed to her knees. She felt numb, as if a hole had opened in her chest where her heart had once been. She saw Lyra's growling face as the great cat pounced!

The girl instinctively threw her backpack in front of her. Sharp teeth sank into the pack like a vise and blue fire exploded around the cat's head. Lyra wailed, shaking her head in pain. The pack tumbled to the ground.

Kara staggered to her feet. The unicorn horn was in her hand. It blazed with power.

Feral eyes turned to the girl, flaring bright with hatred.

"Don't make me do this!" Kara shrieked. Blue fire ran up and down her arms, encircling her.

The cat opened her great wings and rose into the air, razor claws fully extended. With a terrifying roar, she attacked.

"*No!*" Kara screamed, sending every ounce of will into the horn. The fire leaped free and crashed into the cat. For a second, Lyra was held frozen in the air, seared by intense, burning magic.

Something seemed to rip open inside Kara, a deep, bitter pain, screaming for release. And she couldn't stop it. She strained, trying to pull back the power, but it streamed out of her, slamming into the cat.

Lyra was thrown over the rope. For a breathless heartbeat, Kara waited. The wet thud as the cat's body hit sent spasms of sickness racking through her. She couldn't breathe. She wished she would faint. She wanted cool blackness to envelop her, to take her away from the nightmare.

Her heart thundered in her ears as she stumbled to her feet and raced for the trees beyond the riverbank. Kara strained her muscles until they burned and felt like they might rip apart inside her body, but then she was ducking branches, making sharp turns, and diving between narrow clusters of trees.

Kara burst out of the grove, her heart racing, her breath coming in ragged gasps.

Lyra! What had happened? How could she have been so viciously attacked by the one creature on the planet she thought she could trust more than any other?

And now Lyra was dead — killed by her best friend! At last, she fell into her empty house, her eyes burning, and raced upstairs to her room. All she wanted was to hide away forever from the blackness that welled inside, threatening to devour her.

She flung open the door to her bedroom — and froze.

Lyra lay on her bed, amid a pile of stuffed animals and the mad mess of papers and pamphlets for the concert. Her eyes were closed. The cat was *snoring*!

Kara backed away in fear as Lyra's head lazily rose from the pillow. The cat yawned. *"I feel so strange. It's not like me to take a catnap."*

Kara's back hit the door — and she gasped as she accidentally knocked it shut. "Keep away from me!"

Lyra struggled up from the bed, her limbs seemingly heavy with sleep. She looked at Kara with wide, confused eyes. *"Kara, what's happened to you? You're hurt!"*

"Just go!" Kara yelled. "Go!"

Lyra bounded from the bed, her back turned to Kara. *"I don't understand. Did I do something —"*

Kara's chest rose and fell with terror as she slumped to the rug, hands covering her face. "Get out! I don't ever want to see you again!"

Lyra sailed past her, giving one last look of worry and hurt before she leaped out the window. Kara slammed the window shut — and locked it.

Then she collapsed on her bed, reaching into her torn backpack and retrieving the locket that had miraculously not been lost at the bridge.

She cried for a very long time.

☙   ☙   ☙

By the rushing waters of the river, a second winged cat carefully pulled its broken body onto the damp earth. It shook its head and cried out in pain. Then, in a single fluid movement, the creature changed. Animal limbs extended, bones reshaped and straightened becoming long, human legs. Gashes healed as claws turned into fingers. Fur retreated into flesh.

The Skultum stood, carefully examining itself for any other injuries. The girl wielded the power of a unicorn horn! Considering the forces he had seen Kara unleash on the bridge, there could be little doubt now about the girl's ability to do what was required. The blazing star must not be allowed to learn any more than what she already knew. The magic had been meant for Kara alone, but there were two others who knew of the book.

Perhaps he could use this to his advantage.

After all, evil wore many faces and the Skultum could wear any he desired.

Chapter 8

Evening had fallen and Kara had pulled herself together as best she could. She had been lucky. None of the wounds were deep. She bandaged her leg and cleaned the scratches on her arms and sides. She had to tell Emily and Adriane, but she didn't know what to say. It still made no sense. She hid her feelings from Heather, Tiffany, and Molly, who had dropped by with a triple-cheese pizza, to help with the concert preparations. They had no clue that Kara secretly felt her world was coming apart at the seams.

Trying to pretend everything was normal, Kara went into overdrive, making a grand show of flaunting the locket Johnny had given her — which now hung from her neck — regaling her friends with stories of Johnny and his infinite wonder. She was the fearless leader, and she pushed away all the confusion and chaos she felt inside by talking non-stop about the details for Saturday's show, all the time trying her hardest to pretend that her closest friend hadn't tried to rip her to shreds. . . . While Kara sorted through a pile of papers, talking about ticket takers, additional parking, concession stands, placement of banners, and a hundred other things, Heather drifted over to the window and ran through a few simple voice exercises.

Kara kept talking until Tiff and Molly shushed her into silence. When Heather was done, they stared at her in shock.

"That's *amazing,*" Tiffany exclaimed.

"You've been holding out on us, girl!" Molly roared.

They're right, Kara thought. She had never realized how beautiful Heather's voice was.

"How long have you been singing?" Kara asked, looking away and trying to sound like it was no big deal.

"It's no big thing," Heather said modestly, pulling her long red hair back into a ponytail. "You know my mom used to sing, and it gives us something to do together at church."

"Well, tomorrow you're singing at the church of JC," Tiffany quipped. "Johnny Conrad!"

Heather blushed. "You think I really have a chance?"

Tiffany swiveled her hips and shimmied into a

91

dance step. *"Let me tell you, if I sing it true, get up and start the dance,"* she sang, imitating Johnny.

Molly jumped to her friend's side and sang the next verse. *"A rock-and-roll rap with some zap, come on now and take a chance."*

The three girls sang the third verse together. *"No matter what you do, it's your life, you're you."*

They circled Kara and pushed her between them. *"So come on and take a chance and dance!"*

"DANCE! DANCE DANCE! TAKE A CHANCE AND DANCE!" they screamed, hopping and dancing around the room.

"Cut it out!" Kara said, annoyed. She couldn't help thinking of the way she and Lyra had played together in the same way just the other morning.

Molly, Tiffany, and Heather collapsed on the bed in a giggle fit, sending flying pizza remains everywhere.

Only Kara wasn't laughing.

Watching them, Kara felt a sudden flash of jealousy. Heather had natural talent. She could really sing . . . while Kara had to resort to magic. She had borrowed, no — let's get real — *stolen* the unicorn horn.

It was wrong! Or was it . . . ?

Inside, Kara knew she was somehow linked to

the magic. She could be so much more — she had star power!

I don't care if Heather is better than me, Kara thought. *She doesn't want it as much as I do. She doesn't deserve it like I do. . . .*

"C'mon, Heather," Molly squealed, "sing 'Supernatural High,' Be*Tween's song."

Come on, Heather, Kara mimicked Molly in her mind, *let up already, will you?*

Heather started singing.

> *I'm in my moon phase, my pink days*
> *When everything is okay*
> *I am beautiful, invincible*
> *Perfectly impossible*

Kara wished the girl would stop. That was *her* special song. The one she sang with Lyra!

Tiff and Molly barely seemed to notice Kara's distress.

Kara cleared her throat. "*I'm* going over to see Johnny rehearse tomorrow, and then we're doing a radio interview, then Johnny and I, we're gonna —"

Kara had to stop talking as Heather nailed another perfect note.

I can't take anymore, Kara thought. Turning, her

hands over her ears, she shouted, "Heather, will you please stop that noise? It's making me sick!"

Heather stared at Kara in shock. Tiffany and Molly also fell silent.

"Noise?" Heather asked, clearly upset.

Kara stared at Molly and Tiffany. She moved her lips but no words came out.

"Sick?" Tiffany said, springing to her feet and facing Kara. "I'll tell you what's sickening! Hearing you go on and on about how tight you are with Johnny!"

"*Noise* is all the hot air that's been coming out of you ever since this whole concert thing started up!" Molly added.

"This concert thing," Kara repeated, rolling her eyes. "It's *only* to save Ravenswood! Geez. You're all involved in that."

"For you," Molly said in a low, soft voice, shaking her head of short dark hair.

"Yeah," Tiffany said. "My dad says it's no big deal if those animals get shipped off to a zoo or a *professionally* run preserve. It might even be better for them."

"And sometimes it can be a little scary, giving tours with that wolf and that big cat wandering around," Heather noted.

Kara stiffened. "Fine!" she yelled, scattering

the entire pile of papers against the wall with a wide swing of her hand. She couldn't bear to think about the way Lyra had attacked her today. She could still smell the sweet scent of the cat in the room — and she burst into tears.

"Kara, are you all right?" Molly asked.

Kara gave a sharp nod, quickly wiping her eyes. "If you three have better things to do, then don't let me stop you."

Heather picked up the papers and gently handed them back to Kara. "Here. We'd better go."

Kara grabbed the papers and turned away. "Like I said, there's the door, it's not hard to figure out how it works."

Heather pinned Kara with her intense gaze. "Ever since you got involved with Ravenswood, you've changed, Kara! I wish we never heard of Ravenswood!"

Kara felt like she was watching through someone else's eyes as her friends filed out of the room. They were all turning their backs on her! Or was she sending them away?

She slammed the door shut. "Fine. I can do this without you. I don't need anyone!"

A moment later, a knock came at the door.

Ha, Kara thought. *That didn't take long.*

She was certain that when she opened the

door, she would find Heather and the girls looking all upset, and ready to apologize for their selfishness. Instead, she was confronted by Emily.

For an instant, she felt a twinge of guilt — and worry. Had Emily or Adriane realized she'd taken the unicorn horn?

No, that didn't appear to be it. Emily didn't look like she was angry, just a little distracted.

Kara bent to collect what was left of the mass of papers she'd strewn about a few minutes ago. "Emily! Good! I — we have a lot of work to do."

"I can't do any concert stuff tonight," Emily said. "That's not why I'm here."

Kara slumped on the bed, tears threatening to spill once again. She wanted so much to tell Emily about the craziness with Lyra . . . but instinct told her to keep silent. She didn't understand it, but the moment she opened her mouth to speak about the incident, it was as if her throat started closing with panic, her chest seizing up.

Emily sat beside her. "What's wrong, Kara?"

"Nothing. Just a weird day."

"Listen, I've been reading this book we found and —"

Kara was stunned. Did Emily know what she had been up to?

"We have to be really careful with this stuff."

Emily dug into her bag. "Look, I photocopied part of the spellsinging book for you. I'll give Adriane another part and look through the rest myself." She handed some pages to Kara. "If this is what the Fairimental was talking about, then it's important," she added. "We need to read it and then combine our notes, figure out what to do with it."

"Why did they choose us?" Kara asked quietly.

"What do you mean?"

"Why did the Fairimentals have to choose us? They've ruined my life!" Kara wailed. "Everything was fine before I got involved with Ravenswood and this magic stuff!"

"Kara, I don't know why it's us. . . . It just is," Emily said softly. "Now it's up to us to decide what we're going to do about it."

"Like how? How far is this going to go?"

"I don't know," Emily said truthfully. "I think about that a lot, too. Kara, I believe we're each being tested. You remember what Adriane told us about the Prophecy of Three?"

"Yes." Kara did. The Fairimentals had told Adriane about the Prophecy in the Fairy Glen on Aldenmor.

One will follow her heart
One will see in darkness
One will change completely and utterly

"Adriane followed her heart when she went after Storm on Aldenmor. I saw in darkness when I led us across the magic web and back home to Ravenswood. . . ."

"So . . . the third one is mine," Kara said, eyes opening wide. "One will change completely. . . . But I don't want to change!"

Emily took Kara's hand. "Your magic is different than the rest of ours. It's special. We all know that. And we'll stick by you no matter what happens." Emily smiled.

Kara gave her a quick smile in return. "I'd better not change into a flobbin!"

The two friends laughed.

"I have to go," Emily said. "But look over the spells and we'll meet tomorrow at the glade to talk about what we do next. Okay?"

"Okay."

Emily gave Kara a quick hug, then left.

Kara knew she should come clean about the unicorn horn, but she still needed it. She couldn't part with it yet. She looked over the pages Emily had copied for her. There were pages of spells and lessons on how to use singing to control magic. *Here's an interesting one: Spell of Silence — I'd like to use that on Adriane,* Kara mused.

Then she thought about the power she had unleashed behind the school. If her one little rhyme had held such power, especially when combined with the unicorn horn, maybe these real spells could help her make the finals.

She wished she could get her hands on the book itself. But this would have to do.

It looked like everything was going to turn out all right after all.

Chapter 9

The preliminary auditions were held at the school auditorium. After running through a half-dozen outfits, Kara settled on a long beige cardigan over a dark mini, black tights, and her new Valero boots; one moment she thought the outfit looked stylish beyond compare — the next, she was convinced it was hideous. But Kara hadn't been truly satisfied with anything she'd tried on: Nothing would be good enough, Kara was beginning to think . . . especially herself.

Even more frustrating, she had gone through every page that Emily had copied for her of the spellsinging book and hadn't been able to find a single rhyme that was specifically designed to make her magically enhanced singing voice last. The rhymes . . . the *spells* . . . all seemed to have been created for some other purpose. She had tried to sing as soon as she had gotten up, but had found that her voice was back to normal — horrible! She would have to take the unicorn horn with her again.

Lurking around the backstage wings now, Kara stole quick peeks at the audience. Inky Toon, who was presiding over this round of the competition, was chitchatting with reporters. Johnny was talking with folks in the front row, mostly members of the Town Council and their families, along with teachers and a few representatives of the school board. TV cameramen and Web cam operators had set up their equipment to capture the entire event.

When Johnny suddenly turned and looked right at Kara, a half dozen photographers automatically swung around with him and aimed their cameras toward the darkened stage. A barrage of flashes pinned Kara against the curtain, blinding her for a moment. They weren't bright enough to prevent her from making eye contact with Johnny. The instant their gazes met, her fear melted away, replaced by her excitement at all the possibilities he'd offered. She produced her perfect Kara smile for the crowd.

It was as if she was under Johnny's spell every time he looked her way. Touching the locket he had given her, she felt more determined than ever to be a winner and make him proud. Every one of the girls she had talked with backstage had recognized the good-luck charm she wore as Johnny's. A picture of it had appeared in his authorized biography and had been on many of his fan Web sites and in a slew of music magazines.

Some of the girls who recognized it were just excited, and wanted to touch it, or try it on — not that Kara would let them. Several others really were jealous, and shot daggers at her for wearing the locket at all.

Good, Kara thought. Maybe some of them would get psyched out, and that would make it easier for her.

Closing her eyes and leaning against a back wall, Kara smiled. The din created by techies racing around making last-minute checks on the microphone and karaoke equipment simply didn't phase her. Nor did the collective roar of all the nervous contestants who chatted away among themselves.

Touching Johnny's locket, Kara actually felt like she had a chance against her competitors!

A light knocking made Kara open her eyes. She was startled to see Adriane standing before her wearing a black leather jacket and skirt, a black tube top, and black leather boots. Her hair, glistening with subtle red highlights, looked amazing.

"Hey," Adriane said.

Kara nodded. "You look . . . good."

"Thanks, I just, um . . ." Adriane frowned. "We need to talk."

Kara hesitated, a sudden pang of guilt jabbing her . . . then she shrugged. "Now? Can't this wait till later?" she asked impatiently, looking past Adriane to where the contestants were starting to line up.

Kara had drawn her lot when she first arrived. She was number twenty-three. Thank goodness she didn't have to go first!

"No, we can't," Adriane grimaced. "Listen, Kara, I know you've been really . . . busy lately."

"So?"

"*So*, we all need to work together if we're going to figure out how to help the Fairimentals," Adriane insisted.

Kara restrained her urge to agree with Adriane. She wanted to trust her friend . . . but some instinct told her not to let her guard down.

"The thing is," Adriane said, "maybe I've pushed too far, making you go through with this. I don't want to compete with you . . . I mean, let's just call a truce before —"

Kara stared at Adriane cautiously. "Before what?"

"Well . . . before something else happens," Adriane whispered, adding, "I've heard you sing, you know."

Anger flared within Kara. "And you're worried I'm gonna embarrass myself?"

Adriane threw her hands up. "This contest . . . it was *never* supposed to be about the *two of us*. This is for Ravenswood. You're the president, our leader. If you go out there and —"

"That's it," Kara said, her cheeks flushing crimson. She pushed past Adriane to join the others.

"I didn't mean it like that!" Adriane called.

Kara stopped listening. She took her place in line and saw both Adriane and Heather take their places close to the front. Good. She didn't want to deal with either of them right now. She was nervous enough as it was — and Adriane trying to psych her out. . . . That was really too much to deal with.

As the music started and the curtain went up, Kara noticed two of the other girls casting worried looks at her locket. Suddenly feeling like a prize creep, Kara slipped the locket under her blouse, hiding it from view. *A minute ago, I thought it was cool showing it off. What's happening to me?*

Then the show kicked off!

The waiting — and the watching — turned out to be a lot harder than Kara had expected. One by one, boys and girls took the stage, and some were *really* good. Much better than Kara . . . and Kara knew it.

Adriane performed a cover of a classic rock-and-roll song, and she was extraordinary! Kara twiddled with the locket again. Then Inky was on-stage again, introducing "lucky" number seven — Heather Wilson. Heather started to sing and the entire auditorium fell silent. Everyone backstage was buzzing — even Adriane — saying Heather not only had it in the bag to be one of the finalists, but that she would be the one to beat on Saturday during the preshow! Kara noticed several of the girls who were scheduled to go on after Heather walk away from the line and bow out. Others were asking to have their numbers reassigned. It seemed no one wanted to face the humiliation of following Heather's amazing performance. Kara saw Inky nodding and laughing, hanging on to her every note. Even Johnny was enthusiastically caught up in the performance!

Kara knew she should support her friend but she just couldn't bring herself to care. Instead, she drew comfort from the warmth of Johnny's locket.

"Ms. Davies! You're up next!" One of the teachers rushed over to her.

Kara allowed the teacher to lead her to her place in front of the handful of remaining girls. She nervously rubbed the locket around her neck. Several of the other girls looked at her locket once again — and she thought about putting it away.

Then she saw Johnny sitting in the first row, front and center, staring right at her with his bright, winning smile. His eyes flashed with blue fire.

No, she thought. *Why should I hide it? This is my lucky charm!*

Kara was ushered onto the stage, sweaty and shaking. The bright lights seared her eyes as she heard the music start up. It was one of Johnny's hits, a song she knew by heart. And so far tonight, she had been the only one to pick this song.

Two points for me, she thought, terrified. She looked out into the audience and felt her head go light, her knees threaten to turn to water. Just about everyone she knew was watching her, waiting for her to mess up. . . .

Well, to heck with that! Kara thought. Raising her head defiantly, she took the microphone, praying there wouldn't be some embarrassing feedback squawk, or that her voice would keep from breaking as she opened her mouth and prepared to sing her first line. She looked at Johnny, and saw his lips moving, as if he were singing the first verse himself.

And then —

The world stopped. There was a sudden heat at her throat, a fire where the amulet hung. For just a moment Kara experienced a sudden silence, a vacuum that drew all light and sound and sensation from her. She thought she was passing out.

No, this can't be happening!

Then . . . everyone was clapping. Kara shuddered, feeling disoriented and confused. She wondered why the music had stopped, and why she was being showered with applause.

She was still on her feet. She hadn't passed out, clearly. But . . . looking around, Kara saw everyone cheering, and Inky coming out to take the microphone from her.

"But . . ." she whispered, confused and yet feeling — all right, somehow. Like everything was fine.

"You rocked, girl! Totally cool," Inky said.

She'd had some kind of blackout, it seemed. She'd sung the song, and apparently did an okay job — she just couldn't remember doing it.

Weird!

"Kara Davies, everyone!" Inky said. "Everyone, give it up for contestant number twenty-three, Kara Davies!"

The applause rose and Kara bowed, grinning as she felt the adoration of the crowd seep into her like a physical thing, a comforting warmth. She could certainly get used to this part.

Just before she left the stage, she saw Johnny wink at her.

Backstage, Adriane glared at her suspiciously, but Kara didn't care. She had a really good feeling about how things had gone . . . even if she could not exactly remember the event.

The next hour passed in a blur. The other girls did their numbers, with Inky off in the corner, making notes about them. Then he took the stage and announced the finalists.

Heather had made the cut, *duh* there. But so had two girls Kara barely knew, along with Adriane, and —

"Our fifth finalist, Kara Davies!" Inky roared.

Kara raced out onto the stage, thrilled to be part of the winner's circle. She posed with the others for photographs, and Inky said he hoped to see everyone tomorrow — with a healthy donation for the preserve, of course!

Kara was ecstatic — for all of about five seconds.

Before she could say a word, Adriane grabbed her arm and yanked her aside.

"Okay," the tall, slender girl said. "I don't know how you did it, and I don't care."

"Did . . . did what?" Kara asked.

"You went out there and you didn't stink," Adriane said bluntly. "That's great."

"Yeah, thanks," Kara said. "I had so much encouragement from my *friends*." She delivered that last word like an icy dagger.

"And some help, too, no doubt!"

"What do you mean?" Kara asked innocently.

"I mean — this!" Adriane held up her wrist. The wolf stone was pulsing with strong amber light. "I know you used some kind of magic! Don't deny it!"

"No way."

"You cheated!" Adriane hissed. "You took unfair advantage from the start and you shouldn't have been allowed to enter the contest!"

"My singing was just as good as yours," Kara countered.

"In your dreams. You're bowing out of the finals!"

Kara stared at Adriane in absolute fury. "You've gotta be kidding!"

One look into Adriane's eyes — and Kara knew she was deadly serious.

"Wait!" she exclaimed. "I have to be in the finals!"

"Kara, this is about Ravenswood!" Adriane said. "The spotlight needs to be on the preserve, the animals, what we're trying to do for them . . . not about you."

"So why aren't you backing out?" Kara asked. "You cheated, too! You used magic to get the home-court advantage. You've got Johnny practically living right next door. You think people aren't going to talk about that if you win?"

"I haven't been getting Johnny's attention every single minute. You have. I mean . . . look at what you're wearing!"

Shaking with rage, Kara moved to slip the locket out of sight once more . . . then changed her mind.

"Fine! But if I can't sing in the contest, neither can you!" Kara said to Adriane's face. "Or I'll tell everyone how you practiced with Johnny at Ravenswood!"

Adriane looked furious.

"Do we have a deal?" Kara asked.

"Fine! I don't want to be in this stupid contest anymore!" And she stormed off.

Kara turned her back on Adriane and went to talk with Inky. He wasn't exactly happy to hear that she was withdrawing, but there were backup choices for the contest, and so long as this is what Kara really wanted . . . well, then he'd be fine with it.

So maybe she wouldn't sing with Johnny as the contest winner, Kara thought.

There were plenty of other ways to get even for what Adriane had pulled. She looked in her backpack at the photocopies.

Plenty of other spells, too.

Chapter 10

Kara didn't sleep at all that night. Now it was morning — *the* morning, the concert was *today* — but she couldn't get out of bed. She lay buried under blankets and pillows.

It was just so weird . . . why couldn't she remember singing that song?

Maybe it was like one of those things she'd read about. . . . People getting so nervous about a thing that they blank it out of their minds. Except — the song had gone so well. Kara could recall exactly how it felt to stand in front of all those people, to be under the glaring lights, to hear their applause — but that was it. Her mind had taken a shortcut, leaping right over the part that was really difficult, headed right to the instant reward she had craved.

Which . . . wasn't bad, right? Somehow, she really had delivered on that song, and if things had gone the way they should have, the way they were meant to, she would have netted that spot singing with Johnny. Only — Adriane had discovered her secret, part of it, anyway. That Kara had used magic to cheat her way to winning.

Kara was furious with Adriane, but at the same time, she also felt relieved. She hated lying and she hated being a cheater! What had possessed her to even consider such a stupid thing? What would her parents and friends think of her if they knew? She chewed her lip. And the way she had treated Heather . . . that was so cruel. To top it off, she had skipped classes, even destroyed school property! No wonder she hadn't slept much.

Well, it's all over! Am I a girl or a mouse? She tossed the pillows, kicked away the blankets, and sprang out of bed. She would meet Adriane and Emily at the portal field as they had agreed, use the dragonfly phone, and contact Zach. Then she would spill it all and beg her friends to forgive her. She would return the horn immediately before something really dangerous happened. She would forget singing onstage with Johnny and get back to what was really important: getting the word out to the world about Ravenswood!

Someone knocked at her door. "Hey, sleeping beauty!" her father called. "You've got a visitor!"

"I'm not here!" Kara replied. A visitor. Probably Molly or Tiffany . . .

"Not here?" came another voice, light and musical, from downstairs. "Not even for me?"

It was Johnny!

Flying into a pile of clothes, she threw on a pair of jeans and a T-shirt. She yanked open the door, barreled past her startled father, bolted down the steps, then stopped short. Johnny was standing in her living room. Wavy black hair brushed his forehead — his gorgeous blue eyes twinkled.

He grinned. "Ready for the big day?"

Kara nervously ran her hand through her hair, which she knew was a total mess. "Um, uh . . . sure," she said, accompanied by a self-conscious little laugh.

"I have a feeling this is going to be a day people will talk about for years to come." His melodic tones filled her with confidence.

Kara smiled back. Cool.

"So, what's up?" she asked.

"Inky tells me you've decided to back out of the competition."

"Uh, yeah . . ." How was she going to explain this one?

"That's just like you, you know," Johnny said, moving past her to examine the family photos on the fireplace mantle. "Always thinking of your friends first. I have something for you," he added.

Kara waited. The locket Johnny had given her suddenly became warm. Her skin tingled and she tried to stay cool — but suddenly, it was hard to think straight.

"I wrote a song for you," Johnny said.

Kara practically stopped breathing. "You what?"

Johnny took a thin sheet of paper from his pocket. "I wrote it originally for Be*Tween. You know, Inky manages them, too. We're pretty sure it's going to be a number one hit. The problem is — Be*Tween's missing. The way I heard it, they wanted a little time off."

Kara's heart thundered as she scanned the lyrics. He had to be kidding . . . but the look in his eyes was icy calm, deadly serious. This wasn't a gag.

"It's called 'Open the Door,'" Johnny explained. "It's about tearing down walls and letting friends know who you really are inside."

"Why me?" Kara asked.

"First of all, you were great last night," Johnny said. "And second, it's the least I can do for all the work you've done organizing and putting together the concert. And like I said before, you've got something . . . special."

Kara thought of the unicorn horn. Then she felt the heat of Johnny's locket. . . . She felt light-headed and the thought went out of her head.

"And I want you to sing the song tonight, for the first time, during the concert," Johnny said.

"Wow!" A brand-new Johnny Conrad song, and Kara was going to debut it tonight! "But what about the contest?"

"Don't worry about that," Johnny answered her. "We'll get that over with early on. You're going to be the showstopper!"

Kara just couldn't believe it.

"You know what being a star is?"

"What?" Kara whispered.

"When you shine brighter than anyone else in the world."

Kara smiled, eyes wide.

"Brief, bright . . . and then it's over."

"Not for you, Johnny," Kara said, holding her breath.

"Oh, yes, even for me. I'm just this month's musical flavor. A year from now, no one will have ever heard of Johnny Conrad. I'll be yesterday's news."

"No *way*!"

He smiled sadly. "There will be someone newer, cooler. It's just the way it is. But while we *are* stars, we do our best to shine, shooting across the heavens in a blaze of glory! You get all you can, any way you can! And tonight your star will blaze brighter than anyone else's!"

Kara was speechless. She was a blazing star. Is

that what it meant? To flame brighter than anyone else — only to burn out in a blaze of glory? She shuddered.

❀   ❀   ❀

"Blaze!"
"Barney!"
"Fiona!"
"Fred!"
"Goldie!"

Adriane, Emily, Balthazar, Ozzie, Storm, and Ronif moved through the large empty field calling the names of Kara's favorite dragonflies. Although usually complete pests, the magical, flying minidragons were useful at times. They had woven the dreamcatcher that protected the portal to Aldenmor from strands of the magic web. They could also open a small window to Aldenmor. The girls called it a dragonfly phone.

But without Kara the dragonflies were not showing up.

"One thing I can say about her," Adriane grumbled. "She's consistent."

The early morning mist had evaporated from the tall grass, revealing the deep woods of the preserve that lay beyond the field.

Emily looked at her watch again. Nine o'clock. Kara was an hour late.

"All right," she said. "We need another plan."

"It's useless," Ozzie complained. *"Those dragon-flies will only come to Kara!"*

Adriane turned to Storm. "Storm, do you think you can reach out and call to Moonshadow?"

"The wolfsong is strong, but not strong enough on its own to cross between worlds."

Emily's face brightened. "Maybe we can use the dreamcatcher."

"The wolves did contact me through the portal once before," Storm said.

"But how do we open the portal?" Balthazar asked.

"The magic of Lorelei's horn can open it," Emily said.

"I don't think we want to do that," commented Ozzie.

"Maybe the portal doesn't even need to be opened!" Adriane exclaimed, eyes shining. This dreamcatcher is made of the magic web itself." She turned to Storm. "The web might amplify your call."

"Then how do we call upon the dreamcatcher without opening the portal?" Ronif asked.

"With this," Emily said, looking through the pages from the spellsinging book she had taken from her backpack. She handed pages to Adriane and some to Ozzie.

"I saw 'Summoning Spells' in here the other

night," she said. "Try and find them. Maybe we can use one to summon the dreamcatcher."

"All right," Adriane said, looking through the pages. "Beats standing around waiting for Goldilocks." Considering the way Kara had been acting lately, the last thing Adriane wanted to admit was that they actually needed her.

"*Here's one,*" Ozzie exclaimed. "*Say it loud but reverse the words, you'll speak in tongues from a mirror's curve.*"

"That's a backward spell, Ozzie," Emily said. "Makes everything you say come out backward."

"Oops. I have enough trouble just being a ferret!"

"*Float like a cloud, so high, so light,*" Adriane read. "*Hear these words and fly like a kite.*"

"Lightness of Being Spell," Emily said. "Makes you lighter than air."

"Can't wait to try *that* one out on Rapunzel," Adriane giggled.

Emily gave her a stern look.

"You're right," Adriane commented. "She'd just put designer cement in her boots."

"Here." Emily found the page she had been looking for and scanned the text. "*Come to us, so strong and clear. We use this song to bring you near. We summon you before us, the image we see inside. We need your power, by this spell, abide.*"

"Sound okay to you?" Adriane asked, looking to the others.

"If we all focus on the dreamcatcher, it might work," Balthazar said.

"Just one last thing," Emily said. "These spell-songs can only be used *once*. After we use it, we'll forget how it goes, and the words will disappear from the book, and probably from these pages, too. I read that in the introduction."

"Okay, so we get one shot. Let's add some rainbow and wolf power to the mix," Adriane said, holding up her wrist and exposing her wolf stone.

"Okay." Emily held her rainbow jewel next to Adriane's jewel. A spark of magic jumped between the stones, connecting them.

"You take it, Adriane." Emily handed the page to her friend.

"Okay." Adriane started humming a small phrase from a familiar song and then added the lyrics of the spell.

"Come to us, so strong and clear. We use this song to bring you near. We summon you before us, the image we see inside. We need your power, by this spell abide."

At first, nothing happened. The wind stirred a little, then died down. Adriane had reached the end of the song, but the words were still fresh in her mind, the characters still printed on the pages.

"Once more," Emily said to Adriane. She

turned to the others. "Picture the dreamcatcher in your minds. Focus."

Adriane nodded and sang again, and this time — the air began to swirl faster. Winds blew across the grass. Adriane looked down — the words were vanishing from the page. They had done it right!

The air filled with twinkling lights as a giant shape took form in front of them. And a dreamcatcher sparkled, hanging in the sky! The intricate weavings of threads caught the light of the rising sun and sparkled like a thousand diamonds. A circle opened in the center.

"We did it!" Ronif yelled.

"Hurry, Storm," Emily said. "I don't know how long the spell will last."

The silver wolf stood in front of the dreamcatcher and raised her silver-maned head majestically. She howled into the morning sky. In response, the dreamcatcher gently fluttered.

Then Adriane threw back her head and howled with her friend.

Mist filled the circle in the center of the dreamcatcher.

"Again!" Adriane called out. Storm howled her wolf song filled with the spirit of thousands of years of wolf memories.

Suddenly, another howl cut through the morning air, echoing across the field.

"*Moonshadow!*" Storm called out. "*Hear me!*"

The group gathered and peered into the dreamcatcher's center.

The mist began to clear and they saw darkness. It seemed to be nighttime. Dimly, they saw tree-covered hills spreading into the distance. Dark shapes moved.

"*Moonshadow,*" Storm called out again.

A giant black wolf head slid into the misty picture, bright green eyes aglow. "*Stormbringer! My heart fills with happiness!*"

"*As does mine, my wolf brother,*" Storm answered.

"*There is so — arrg!*" A blond head of hair shoved the big wolf aside. Zach's face filled the window.

"Adriane! Are you there, too?" Zach called out.

"Zach! It's me!" Adriane's heart flew with joy at the sight of her friend. "Are you all right?"

"Yes. We're at the Packhome*gahh —*" Zach was shoved out of the window by the huge black wolf.

"*There is much to say and not much time,*" Moonshadow warned.

"Tell us," Emily called.

"*The Black Fire has stopped raining from the skies.*"

"That's good news!" Adriane exclaimed.

Zach shoved in next to his wolf brother, angling for position. "We thought so, at first. We've been camped on the foothills near the Shadowlands, sending in scouting teams."

He looks tired, Adriane thought. She wished she could sit beside him, comfort him, talk and laugh with him like she had done on Aldenmor. She tried to ignore the sadness welling in her chest. "What is the Dark Sorceress up to now?" she asked.

"She's planning something big!" Zach told them. "She has completed building four giant crystals. We think they have been designed to hold magic, lots of it."

"Aldenmor grows barren of magic. We fear for the Fairimentals!" Moonshadow howled sadly. The howls of his pack mates echoed behind him.

"If there is so little magic left on Aldenmor, then why has she built these crystals?" Balthazar asked.

"She means to draw magic from somewhere else," Zach said worriedly.

No one had to ask where that might be. There was only one place that held the kind of magic the Sorceress desired. The home of all magic: Avalon.

"We know the Sorceress damaged sections of the web trying to do something to the portals," Emily said. "She even tried to use the magic of a unicorn horn, but it wouldn't work for her."

"Yeah, so how is she going to succeed this time?" Adriane asked.

Zach was silent for a few seconds. "She has the

fairy map to show the sequence of portals that lead to Avalon."

"I, too, carry a fairy map, of Aldenmor, given to me by my human wolf sister!" Moonshadow managed to stick his nose in.

Adriane smiled. "It was a gift from the Fairimentals. I just brought it to you from them."

"Wait!" Emily said. "We know that you can only use fairy magic if it's given to you. The Sorceress stole that fairy map. She can't use it."

"But there is one person it was meant for," Ozzie said, almost to himself. *"Who can use it."*

Emily and Adriane knew. "Kara," they said at the same time.

"The dreamcatcher is fading," Ronif yelled.

"Be careful," Zach said, talking faster. "The Sorceress may have sent someone to your world to get Kara to use it for her."

"Someone new *did* show up at Ravenswood recently . . ." Emily began.

"Yeah, someone who *volunteered* to come," Adriane continued.

"Someone who Kara is spending an awful lot of time with . . ." Emily added.

"Johnny!" Adriane finished.

"Adriane, whatever happens here," Zach called out, "you cannot allow Kara to use that fairy map!"

"Yes," Adriane said. "Stay strong, Zach. I prom-ise we will see you and the wolves again. Soon! And you'd better be right at the portal when I get there!" She had to fight back her tears.

Zach smiled, his green eyes warm and full of light as he faded away.

The dreamcatcher was vanishing, sparkling lights twinkling back into mist.

Suddenly, a mighty howl rose from the entire wolf pack, reaching across the worlds. Adriane and Storm howled back, cementing their bond with the promise of hope.

🌀 🌀 🌀

Later, Emily headed for Kara's house, in case Kara was still at home but not answering her phone, getting ready for the concert.

Adriane went straight back to the manor.

"Adriane!" Gran was standing in the open doorway of their cottage, waving. "Come here a moment!"

"Can it wait?" Adriane asked, pausing on the cobblestone pathway. "I'm kind of in a hurry."

"This will just take a minute. I need to show you something."

Shrugging, Adriane turned and followed her grandmother into the house.

"What's up?" she asked as they entered the liv-ing room.

"I don't feel so good," Gran told her, pointing at the couch.

Adriane spun around — and was shocked to see . . . her *grandmother* lying on it? She heard the front door lock behind her.

"Huh?" Adriane whirled around to face the "other" grandmother, who was smiling sweetly. There were *two* Grans. But that was impossible!

"This is where you're supposed to say: 'My, what sharp teeth you have, Grandmother.'" The imposter leaned toward her with a little snicker.

Before Adriane could react, the old woman sprang at her with a strength and speed that Adriane would have thought impossible — if she'd had the chance to think at all. She was too busy screaming as her grandmother's face changed. For a brief moment, Adriane thought she was looking at Johnny, and then, the creature's skin turned green and scaly, fingernails turned to talons, teeth grew sharp and long, and the eyes blazed with a terrible inhuman fire.

"Time for a little nap, dear," the Skultum said, its huge hands covering Adriane's face.

Adriane felt tingling magic sink deep into her as she caught a sudden, terrifying glimpse of the creature's form changing once more, becoming a perfect duplicate of Adriane herself. Then all was black.

Chapter 11

Rows of people stretched all the way down the driveway leading into Ravenswood Preserve, in line for the concert. Behind the manor, those already there wandered in the crisp afternoon sun. Families strolled with children, kids and teens hung out, music filled the air, blasting from the stage set on the great lawn. The entire town had shown up. Kara had heard upward of three thousand people were in attendance, not huge by stadium standards, but a smashing success for Stonehill and for Ravenswood. Concession stands were doing brisk business selling popcorn, hot dogs, and soda. Everyone wore Ravenswood T-shirts, sweatshirts, hats, and bandannas. There were even small, stuffed toys of favorite Ravenswood animals, Ariel, Storm, Ozzie, and Lyra.

A huge banner hung behind the stage. The words SAVE RAVENSWOOD! were stenciled over an image of a giant dreamcatcher. That had been

Adriane's idea. Kara wished she had thought of it first.

Kara wandered, waving to the crowds spread out across the great lawn. *This is going unbelievably well,* she thought. Sporting a Ravenswood hat and shiny dreamcatcher lapel pin, she looked great in her new cords, boots, and brand-new brown suede jacket worn over her Ravenswood T-shirt. So why did she feel like a total loser? She knew exactly why. Although she had learned Johnny's new song, she was torn between using the magical help of the unicorn horn and just being herself, no matter what she sounded like. The pressure of debuting a Johnny Conrad original was unbearable! She had never felt so nervous, so out of sorts. How could she *not* use the magic!

"Kara!"

It was her dad. Mayor Davies was standing with the Town Council. A group of reporters were interviewing them near the side of the stage. The mayor was waving to her. "Kara, honey! Over here!"

Kara trudged over as a woman reporter moved to intercept her.

"Ms. Davies," the reporter beamed. She stuck the mike in Kara's face.

"What's your message to the world about Ravenswood?"

Kara thought hard. All those long months of planning, all the worry, the problems, the dreams had all come down to these few moments. Images of her friends flashed through her mind. Emily, Adriane, Molly, Heather, Tiffany . . . the animals, Ozzie, Storm, and once upon a time, Lyra.

"Ravenswood is more than just a wildlife preserve," she said at last. "It's . . . it represents our whole planet. We share our world with animal friends who count on us, and we count on them. And with help from all our friends, we can make our world a better place for everyone."

"Well said." The reporter was clearly impressed. "I'm putting this on the national feed," she told an elated council.

"The whole world will soon see what a fine example you have set for young people everywhere," the reporter said, shaking Kara's hand.

Kara stiffened. What if the whole world saw that she was a cheater? "Um, thank you," she said uncomfortably. She had to get out of here — and take care of this once and for all. "Dad, I have to go . . . check on some final details."

"Okay, honey." The mayor didn't miss a beat, continuing to smile and talk proudly about Stonehill's future, as Kara slipped away.

"A fine example for young people everywhere . . ." What a crock! She *had* to fix this. Clutching her backpack tight against her chest, she hurried through the laughing crowds and snuck in through the back door of the manor house.

She scurried up the stairs to the library. She would do what she had come here to do. She would do what was right — put the magical unicorn horn back. And whatever happened onstage later when she sang would happen. At least she would do it on her own. She was through with the cheating, the lying. In the end, she knew, she had only deceived herself.

She reached the library door and was surprised to find it unlocked and open a crack. Then she heard sounds from within. *Click-clack. Tap-tap-tap.*

Someone was using the computer!

Kara grabbed the knob and swung the door open, ready to ask Emily or Adriane why they were in there with the door unlocked when so many strangers had free run of the mansion.

But it wasn't Emily or Adriane at the computer. It was Johnny.

Johnny Conrad sat at the keyboard to their secret computer, weird images flickering on the screen before him. He looked over at Kara and grinned. "Hey, what's up?"

"I — I —" she stammered. Trying to mask her surprise, she ran her hands through her mane of blond hair. "What are *you* doing in here?"

The computer was way off-limits to anyone but the girls. The information locked away held all kinds of files about . . . magic.

Johnny looked confused. "I was just checking my E-mail. Adriane told me it would be okay. What, did I do something wrong?"

Worried that someone else might walk in, Kara swung the door closed behind her. Johnny seemed relaxed and confident as ever, not at all like someone who was about to perform in front of thousands of people . . . in about ten minutes! "Aren't you supposed to be, like, in your dressing room, getting ready?"

"I don't have a dressing room. This isn't exactly the Staples Center, you know," he joked. "Hey. Check this out. I found the Ravenswood Website. There's a live Web feed of the whole event."

Kara walked over and stared at the screen. A window was opened. It displayed a live camera view of the stage and great lawns. Had Johnny seen her walking to the manor?

"Adriane also showed me all these cool files you've set up for your Website." Johnny swung back around and hit some keys. Pictures of the animals appeared in windows. "It's really great."

Kara drew a sharp breath. Crossing her arms over her chest, Kara cautiously came closer and got a better look at the screen. *Had Adriane completely lost her mind? The girls had made a solemn pact to keep the computer secret!*

"So, you all set for your number?" Johnny got up and stretched like a sleek jungle cat. He moved to one of the large windows overlooking the event out back. The window was open, and the sounds of laughter drifted up to the library.

"I guess." Kara frowned as she joined him. They looked out at the vast crowd. Onstage, techies were finishing the last of the sound and light checks. "So . . . Adriane let you in here?" she asked.

"Well, *yeah*." Johnny smiled. Then his gaze narrowed. "What — did you think I picked the lock or something? If I wanted to be sneaky I would have snuck in at, like, three in the morning."

Good point, Kara realized. Yet . . .

"I just don't get why Adriane would do that," Kara said suspiciously. "Some of the things we keep in here are . . . private."

For the first time, Johnny looked uncomfortable. "You and Adriane *are* friends, right?"

"Of course. Why do you ask that?"

Johnny pointed out the open window. Chants and cheers began to rise from the happy crowd. "Johnny! Johnny!"

"Remember what we talked about, about what being a star means?" Johnny asked her.

"Yes." Kara suddenly felt the locket she was wearing grow warmer against her skin.

"Stars have to make sacrifices. Look at the crowd out there. When you're onstage, it's all for them. Giving everything you have."

Kara felt the excitement of performing starting to build.

"They expect the best you can be," Johnny reminded her, "and you have to deliver, no matter what it takes. Not everyone can be a star. Being special, one in a million, means standing alone. It changes everything. People you thought were friends can turn on you, betray you."

The words snaked into Kara's mind. *Adriane has always been jealous of me.*

Johnny looked at her with his deep, dark, soulful blue eyes. "How well do you really know Adriane?"

Kara was taken aback. Had he read her mind? "I've only known her for a few months. . . . Why?"

"When you're a star, friends can do things, act weird. Has anything happened recently? Anything that, I dunno, might have *changed* her?"

Again the locket felt warm against her skin — and suddenly, Kara thought about the time Adriane had spent on Aldenmor . . . and in the Dark Sorceress's dungeon. Was it possible that Adriane had come back *changed*, somehow? That maybe the Dark Sorceress had gotten to her, had made her evil? It would explain why Adriane had been acting like such a little *witch* lately.

"Adriane . . . went away for a little while," Kara said. "She met some not-so-nice people."

"I've seen it before." Johnny rubbed his temples. "Listen, I hate to be the one to tell you this, but it's for your own good."

"What? Tell me," Kara demanded.

"Your friend Adriane has been asking me and Inky, right from the beginning, how she can get a record contract. She wants to sing her own song, which Inky thinks could be a single, onstage at the concert."

Kara flinched. The locket was even warmer now — but nowhere near as fiery as her anger. "What else?"

"She said . . . *she* should be the *Blazing Star*. Not you."

Kara was speechless.

"I . . . I don't believe that," Kara stammered.

Johnny's eyes filled with sympathy. "Well, she's in the ballroom right now rehearsing."

Her brow furrowed in confusion and anger.

She spun around and started pacing. "I cannot believe that girl!" Kara yelled. "She told me she wasn't going to sing onstage. We had a deal!"

Johnny watched her. "I'm sorry. But like I said, when you're a star, friends can turn on you."

The locket flared — Kara was enraged. How could Adriane do this to her?

Spellsinging under his breath so softly she wouldn't hear it, wouldn't detect his lips moving at all, he exerted just enough influence. He had to be careful, even the slightest magic could alert the magic of the horn.

"Why did you come to the library, Kara?"

"Huh? I was going to return something. . . ."

"Remember what I said. You need to use whatever you can to make sure you deliver. You have to shine and show the world that *you* are the blazing star. That's the only way you can beat Adriane." A slight smile played across Johnny's lips.

"Oh, don't worry about that! I am going to blaze so bright the entire audience will need sunglasses." She didn't give another thought to returning the unicorn horn or leaving Johnny alone in the library. Kara stormed out of the room.

The *only* thing she cared about right now was dealing with Adriane once and for all!

Behind her, Johnny Conrad watched her go. A cruel smile appeared on his perfect face.

He sang a little tune and spread his fingers. A twinkling ball of stars winked into existence, floating in midair. He grinned as he stared at the sparkling fairy map, at the bright silver glow in its center . . . so much like a *blazing star*.

"Poor, confused little Kara," Johnny sneered, raising his hand and touching the floating orb. "You have no idea of the power that's inside you."

The little fool. He knew her weaknesses, her vulnerabilities, her needs. . . . She was so pathetically easy to read — and to manipulate. Hardly a challenge at all. The unicorn horn had been a surprise, but that had proved a blessing in disguise. He chuckled at his selection of words.

He had practically *smelled* its power on her. But he could do nothing with it directly. The unicorn horn had been freely given to the Three, and as a result, only Kara, or one of her friends, could unleash its power.

He was, of course, much more powerful than Kara as a spellsinger. But magic was more than spellsinging . . . much more.

And, as he had told her quite honestly, she had something others simply didn't possess. Star power. She would go out like a blazing star, a burst of magical energy as bright as the sun. If anyone's life was going to be sacrificed in this endeavor, it wasn't going to be his. And if by some miracle she

135

survived tonight's events, his instructions were to turn her over to the Dark Sorceress. She would disappear. Just as Be*Tween had disappeared. He pictured the famous girl band. They would never find a way to defeat him or any dark magic again.

With her power — strengthened by her use of the unicorn horn — his song could not fail. "Open the Door" was his greatest creation. Kara would spellsing the words that would unlock the fairy map. With that much power, the portals between this world, Aldenmor, and Avalon itself would open in just the right order, laying the path for the Sorceress to do as she pleased.

He had to make *very sure* that Kara sang her song tonight. The locket could help to sway her, influence her, but it could not control her completely.

There was one final thing left to do, to lock Kara to his will and make her use her magic with enough force to open the portal and trigger the map. Her spirit must be broken.

He smiled, his voice musical, chiming and tremulous. Before him, the fairy map returned to its invisible hiding place. "Places to go, people to be . . ."

Closing his eyes, he stood by the open window. He concentrated, reaching out with his otherworldly senses.

"Show time. Guess I better fly," Johnny said. Throwing his arms open wide, he allowed his form to shimmer and change, to melt as his arms transformed to wings and his body shrank to the size of a large dark bat.

With a flutter of bat wings, the Skultum flew out the window.

Chapter 12

Throwing open the double doors, Kara stomped into the large ballroom. The clip-clop of her boots against the hardwood floor echoed in the empty space. All of the band's equipment had been moved out. The formal dining table, which had been moved to the side, was covered with bottles of water, fresh fruit in large bowls, and platters with meat and cheese, cakes, brownies, and other leftover sweet treats. Drapes covered the immense windows leaving the room dark.

Kara stopped and stared in utter amazement as she saw what hung on the walls. The heavy wood-framed pictures of wilderness scenes were gone. In their place were posters, each featuring Adriane singing, dancing, and playing guitar. They read: #1 WITH A BULLET, HOT HOT HOTTIE, THE NEW MUSIC SENSATION, OOPS, I WIN AGAIN!

Kara was stunned.

Suddenly, a spotlight splashed onto the wood

floor at one end of the room. From the dark shadows, Adriane stepped into the center of it. She was decked out in shiny silver pants, black crop top with the words ROCK'N'ROLL WARRIOR emblazoned on it, silver boots, and sunglasses. Her hair was layered in streaks of red, gold, and pink. She had a sparkling purple metal-flake guitar strapped across her back. With a swift martial arts move, she swung the guitar in position and strummed a loud chord.

The chord filled the room, resonating with power. Kara stood in total shock as Adriane began to sing.

> *One, Two — take a look at you*
> *You're standin' there, you think I care*
> *but don't you know,*
> *Anything you can do,*
> *I can do better.*
> *Three Four — you're such a bore*
> *It's all about me, can't you see*
> *that in the end,*
> *Anything you can do,*
> *I can do better.*

The spotlight followed Adriane as she moved around the room, singing and dancing like a superstar.

"That's enough!" Kara yelled in fury.

Adriane strummed the guitar one more time, then swung it back over her shoulder. "And that's just my warm-up number," she said coolly.

"You look totally. . . . *stupid!*" Kara announced.

Adriane laughed. "You're funny."

Kara crossed her arms. "We had a deal! You said you weren't going to sing in the show," she yelled.

"I said I wasn't going to sing in the contest! You're the one sneaking around getting your own spot! Why shouldn't I get my own spot? I'm so much better than you'll ever be!" Adriane taunted her.

"Are not!" Kara yelled.

"Am too!" Adriane retorted.

"Not!"

"Too!"

"You think all this magic is going to make you a star?" Kara waved her arm around the room.

"Hey, you started it," Adriane said, cruel glimmers of dark delight dancing in her eyes. "You're the one who cheated. You stole the horn."

Kara's face flushed. How had Adriane discovered that?

"So don't lecture me about magic! Cheater!" Adriane snickered.

Kara shook her head. "This can't be happening."

"But it is," Adriane said, walking to the table and taking a swig from a water bottle. She chucked the plastic bottle against the wall and swung her guitar into position. "You know what you are? You're a blazing *dud*! I'm the one who's going to shine tonight!"

"That's my spot and no one is going to take it from me!" Kara said angrily.

Adriane spun around and played a fast series of notes, fingers running up the guitar neck, sending out sounds so loud Kara thought they'd make her head explode — Adriane played faster and jumped, doing a split in the air. She landed, stomping her boots on the floor. A fiery crimson streak of energy ripped from the instrument and slammed into the wall, just missing Kara by inches.

"Hey! This is real suede, you know!"

Adriane strolled to the table and ate a piece of cake while Kara struggled to her feet.

"I don't know what's gotten into you," Kara said quickly, "but there's only one spot open in the show. And that spot is for me!"

Adriane giggled. She gripped her guitar again. "Really? You think you're gonna be up for that, Miss Clueless, or should I say, Miss Jewel-less?"

Kara saw Adriane's lips begin to move, and a soft song rose into the air. Was Adriane *spellsinging*? Then, whirling, Adriane jammed on her guitar,

141

letting loose another volley of crimson bolts at Kara.

But this time, Kara was ready for her. She leaped out of the way, holding up the unicorn horn like a lightsaber.

Desperately, she tried to remember the spell-songs she had seen. The Spell of Silence came to her — but the words were all scrambled. For some reason, she just couldn't remember it right. Other spellsongs flashed in her mind. All she needed was a chance, a few seconds to deliver one of the songs —

"Look at you!" Adriane sneered. "You're magically impaired!"

Kara gripped the horn tight. "Be . . . *quiet!*"

Power rippled through Kara, and Adriane darted back, her fingers moving over the frets in a blur. A crackling red shield of energy appeared around her. The shield buckled in a half-dozen places as the magic from the unicorn horn crashed into it — but it didn't yield.

"What's the problem, Kara?" Adriane asked, her guitar wailing again, crimson sparkles of energy surrounding her. "Can't take the heat? You gonna wimp out onstage, too?"

"Stop it!" Kara commanded. The table rattled with energy. A chocolate layer cake lifted and smashed into Adriane's face, making her gasp in surprise.

Kara laughed.

Wiping off the chocolate, Adriane walked to the table and eyed the bowl of fruit. "Messy, huh?"

Kara's eyes went wide. "Oh no! Don't even think about it!"

Adriane strummed the guitar again. Kara dove into the corner, waving the horn about to defend her clothes from flying fruit, cookies, pretzels, and chips.

Kara stood up triumphant. Then she looked down. There was a big stain right on the front pocket of her new suede jacket! "That's it!" she screamed.

Holding up the horn, Kara sent a blazing arc of blue fire hurtling across the room, smashing into the table, sending food, dishes, and Adriane flying. Adriane landed with a graceless *oomf!* as her crimson shield faded away.

"The truth is, you don't have what it takes," Adriane shot back, rising on wobbly legs. "*I'm* the one Johnny really wants to sing with."

"You are, like, so deluded!" Kara said, raising the horn again. "I'm glad I took the horn!" She tingled with delight — and felt a matching warmth against her heart where Johnny's locket lay — as Adriane's face went pale.

"So I can teach you a lesson," Kara said, advancing on the other girl. "Lesson one: You have no . . . taste!"

Kara waved the horn in a circle like a magic wand, releasing sparkles of magic. The posters glowed with light, and suddenly the pictures of Adriane were all replaced by images of Kara. She was dressed in the coolest outfit, singing and dancing like a star. A blazing star!

Kara smiled in satisfaction.

🌀   🌀   🌀

Carolyn Fletcher drove the green Suburban through the gates of Ravenswood. Emily sat in the passenger seat, nervously looking out the window. Cars were parked along the driveway past the gate and all the way down Tioga Road. Crowds of people were walking toward the back of the preserve, some carrying picnic baskets.

"Look at all these cars," Carolyn commented. "This is really incredible, Em. And all the people! I can't wait to see Mrs. Windor's face when she —"

"Healer!"

Emily jumped against the shoulder strap. "Storm?"

"It's a beautiful day, hon," Carolyn said to her. "No chance of a storm."

"Come quickly!"

"What is it?" Emily frantically scanned the grounds.

"It's just a bit of traffic. Emily, are you all right?"

"Adriane has been hurt! We're at the cottage."

"Mom! Stop the car!"

"What?"

"Let me out! I have to . . . fix something!"

Carolyn pulled the car to the side as Emily bolted out the door. "I'll catch up to you later!" she yelled as she ran across the front lawn to the far side of the manor.

Storm practically bowled her over as she rounded the cobblestone path that ran to the Chardáy cottage. The mistwolf's fur bristled with distress.

"Something's happened to her," Stormbringer said.

Emily burst through the front door. Adriane was on the floor. Gran was on the couch. Emily ran to Adriane and checked her pulse. Then she moved to check Gran.

"Ahhhh!"

Emily swung around at the scream. Ozzie stood in the door, mouth open. He was flanked by Lyra, Ronif, and a few other quiffles. Four pegasii stood behind him along with some brimbees and wommels, all peering into the cottage.

Ozzie ran over and looked into Adriane's face. "She's dead!"

"No, Ozzie," Emily said calmly. "She's sleeping. So is Gran."

Ozzie flopped to the floor. "Thank goodness."

"Adriane. Adriane, wake up!" Emily called. "Storm, what happened?"

"I felt her distress, her fear . . . then nothing."

"Come on, Adriane, rise and shine!" Ozzie murmured, patting the side of Adriane's face.

But, no matter how hard they tried, they couldn't bring Adriane around. Gran was in the exact same state.

"Something is not right here," Emily said. She turned to all the animals that had gathered outside of the cottage.

"Everyone! Inside! Quickly!" Emily commanded. "You're supposed to all be in the glade!"

The animals barreled into the cottage. Although it wasn't a small house, it was soon overstuffed with fur, beaks, flippers, and wings.

"Gather around me," Emily said.

"Gah! That shouldn't be hard!" Ozzie's muffled voice said.

Emily looked around for Ozzie and found him stuck between a wommel and a hard place.

Pulling him free, she settled next to Adriane

and held out her wrist. The rainbow jewel pulsed with blue-green light. Emily concentrated and sent out her healing magic to her sleeping friend. She sensed no physical injury, just a deep blackness. Adriane stirred but did not awaken.

"She's in some kind of deep trance," Ozzie realized.

"A spell," Ronif said.

"Yes . . ." Emily mused, "a spell."

"Everyone concentrate with me," Emily commanded. "Send healing strength to help Adriane."

She focused her jewel and reached out again.

The wolf stone on Adriane's wrist flashed with light. Emily quickly placed her gem next to the wolf stone, willing the healing magic to flow into Adriane. Both gems flared with magic and Adriane's eyes fluttered opened. "Hey," she said groggily. "Is that a ferret in my face?"

❧ ❧ ❧

The Skultum had no idea what was happening. Not at first. He was wearing Adriane's form and had Kara fighting to give it all up onstage, just as he had planned.

Then, he'd suddenly started to feel weak. His entire body trembled, his flesh crawled, and it was hard to keep posing as Adriane.

He was beginning to change. That meant his

victim had awakened, which should have been impossible! The only way that spell could be broken was with . . . magic.

The other young mages would know what was going on — and so would the real Adriane!

Hissing, the Skultum threw down the guitar and stumbled back, his stolen "Adriane" form losing its shape as he looked around for a way out.

Kara gasped. Adriane's face was *changing* . . . no, not just her face, it was the girl's entire form! For a shocking, mind-splintering instant, Kara saw — or *thought* she saw — Adriane morph into Johnny and *become* the singer. His hands danced, fingers moving in complex patterns as a strange song left his lips. Then, in a heartbeat, the figure before her shimmered and transformed into a monstrous creature covered in green scales. Slivered reptile eyes shone from its hideous face. Then it was gone.

"What . . . what just happened?" Kara began, attempting to wrap her thoughts around the horrific thing she had just seen . . . or *thought* she had just seen. . . .

"Ahhouch!" Johnny's locket flared red hot against her skin. She flinched and looked away. Her thoughts grew hazy, her head throbbed. Then the locket cooled and Kara felt a deep sense of triumph and exhilaration. So what if Adriane had gotten away? Kara had proved to Adriane that she was the blazing star, and now she would prove it to the world! Nothing would stand in the way of her singing the big number with Johnny! She *was* a star, baby! A blazing star!

Suddenly, something flew by Kara, flapping down the corridor into which Adriane had somehow disappeared. *Ewww!* A bat! A few seconds later, she heard footsteps behind her and turned to see Johnny entering the ballroom from the entrance across the room.

The singer quickly covered the distance separating them. Concern tinged his words. "Kara, what happened? Are you all right?"

"You were right, Johnny," she told him. "Adriane wanted to sing in the spotlight. She wanted to take my place!"

"Well, don't worry. No one can take your place! I'll make sure Adriane doesn't get anywhere near you during the show."

"Thanks," Kara said, still feeling a little shaky.

Johnny smiled as he led Kara to the back door of the manor and onto the great lawn. The crowd was chanting for Johnny. His band had taken their places onstage, ready to rock.

"It's show time." Johnny straightened his leather jacket as he led Kara to the side of the stage. People covered the entire field.

"Johnny! Johnny!"

"Are you ready?" he asked Kara.

"Kara! Kara!" Did she hear the crowd shouting her name also?

"Yeah!" Kara wiped the dried stain from her jacket. "I'm ready to shine!"

"All right! Let's kick it!"

❧   ❧   ❧

Adriane paced back and forth as Emily entered the living room. "Gran's fine now. Just resting," she reported.

"We were right," Adriane said, her hands balled into fists, wolf stone pulsing. "It's Johnny! Only it's worse than we thought. . . . Whatever he is, he's not human."

"A shape-shifter," Balthazar said.

"That's what we sensed the other night," Ronif added.

"That's bad," Ozzie said

"How bad?" Adriane asked, pacing.

"Worse than a werebeast." Ozzie paced with her. "This one is real cunning. I'd say demon level."

"Kara is in terrible danger!" Lyra was wildly pacing now. *"We have to help her!"*

"You have to get back to the glade!" Emily said, then turned to the rest of the group. "All of you!"

From outside, they heard the sounds of rockin' drums, a thumping bass, and a wild electric guitar.

"The show's started!" Ozzie yelled.

Then the most powerful spellsinging voice in the world rang out. Johnny Conrad had taken the stage.

Chapter 13

*D*ANCE! DANCE! DANCE! TAKE A CHANCE AND DANCE!"

Buzzing with excitement, Kara watched from the wings, as Johnny launched into his opening number. The audience loved it, moving, clapping, dancing to the music. Johnny had them in the palm of his hand.

Kara thought back to how she had first pictured the event, months ago. And now it was really happening! Here she was with Johnny Conrad, about to become a star!

She would use the magic. She had no choice. Her song with Johnny had to go perfectly.

"Kara! Kara!"

Was the crowd calling out her name already? She scanned the rows of faces. They were all intently watching Johnny, center stage.

"Over here!"

Just outside the roped-off area beside the stage, Emily and Adriane were jumping and waving. Adriane was in her black skirt, sweater, and dark green jacket. *When did she have time to change?* Kara wondered.

They were yelling something but she couldn't make it out above the music.

She turned back to the stage as Johnny finished his first song.

"Hello, Stonehill!" the pop star shouted. "It's a great night for Ravenswood!" The audience exploded in applause. Then, the band blazed into their second number. Johnny rocked out, doing the moves that had made him famous.

Kara danced along in the wings, jumping and — *ow!* Something had just bitten her! She spun around but nothing was there. Another spark stung her leg. What was that? Then she caught a telltale flash of amber light. *Zing!* She'd been bitten again! Adriane! Angry, she whirled around and saw the black-haired girl standing, arm raised, golden light flaring from her jewel. Kara narrowed her eyes and stuck her tongue out. She was just starting to turn away when she saw Adriane pointing. Kara followed Adriane's finger. Emily was holding up a sign. IT WASN'T LYRA!

Kara stopped moving. It wasn't Lyra? She loved Lyra more than anyone, but she'd been avoiding the cat. She hadn't even really thought of her since . . . it wasn't Lyra!

153

Something twisted in her stomach. She looked back at Emily again, who now had a second sign raised: IT WASN'T ADRIANE!

What did Emily mean? Lyra and Adriane had been *horrible* to her. Of course it was them! She'd seen them! A tingle of fear crept up Kara's back, tickling its way to her neck. She took a tentative step toward her friends.

Suddenly, the locket around her neck burned with intense heat. Her mind became hazy. Johnny was finishing his second number, but he was looking directly at her, anger flaring across his face. Kara shook her head — she must be crazy! She turned back to the stage and was relieved to see Johnny's look soften before he faced the crowd and bowed.

"Before we continue," he announced, "I know you're all excited about the contest. And I have picked the winner!"

What? Kara's face mirrored the surprise on the contestants' — no one had performed yet!

Johnny continued, "Let's hear it for the person who made this whole day possible, Ravenswood's very own Kara Davies!"

Applause thundered as Johnny beckoned Kara. In a daze, she stepped out onstage.

"And we have a surprise for you — we're going to perform a brand-new song dedicated to the

Ravenswood Preserve!" Johnny smiled at Kara. "Give it all you got!"

He nodded to the band, and the music started. Kara felt light-headed. Would she even remember her performance this time?

The audience sat waiting as the band reached her cue. Kara opened her mouth and sang.

In a world that spins so fast
Can't keep your feet on the floor
Where the future has no past
Open the door, open the door, open the door . . .

Kara scanned the crowd and felt her cheeks flush. Wincing, she spied Heather flanked by Molly and Tiffany, all snickering. This was awful. Kara's voice hadn't changed a bit

"Sing it!" Johnny hissed. "You're the star! Make it happen! Use your star power."

The locket around her neck flared with heat and Kara thought, *When they see what kind of star I am, they'll come back to me.*

She *deserved* to be the blazing star. That was her destiny, and Johnny could make it happen.

Reaching into her jacket, she felt the comforting coolness of the unicorn horn. Gripping it tightly, she called upon its magic . . . and sang.

Opportunity is just a window
So no matter what's in store
Open it up and let it flow
Open the door, open the door . . .

Kara's voice suddenly soared into the air, hitting perfect notes. She sang louder, moving her feet to the backbeat.

Johnny leaped into the air and danced. "That's it!"

The audience cheered.

Open the door, let it flow

As Kara sang the chorus, she could feel the mystical energies flowing from the unicorn horn. Lights behind the stage flashed in time to the beat as a wave of blue light pulsed around her.

Johnny was ecstatic. "Beautiful! More! Give it more! Open the door!"

And she did.

         🌀   🌀   🌀

In the distance, away from the surging crowd, Storm and Lyra ran into the open field. The portal to Ravenswood opened wide, ripping the air with shrieking winds against the darkening horizon. The sparkling dreamcatcher that kept Ravenswood safe stretched across it, strong and ready to amplify any magic sent into it.

Emily and Adriane were pushed to the side of the great lawn as people surged forward to get closer to the stage. *"Warrior! Healer!"* The girls heard the mistwolf's urgent voice.

"What is it, Storm?" Adriane asked.

"There is strong magic in the air. The portal has opened!"

The girls looked back up at Kara and saw the blue glow around her. That wasn't special effects! That was magic!

They pushed and shoved their way to the stage.

"Kara, stop!" Emily called. "You're opening the portal!"

Kara heard them and faltered. But before she could react, there was a blast of heat from the locket — and suddenly, she was singing louder than ever, releasing more and more of the horn's magic.

"Johnny!" Adriane shouted, nodding toward the wildly grinning singer. "He's making her do it!"

And though Kara was singing like an angel, there was pain and fear in her eyes.

The bass thrummed a thumping rhythm, and the band began its instrumental break. Johnny pumped his fist in the air as he swaggered across the stage, drawing the crowd to their feet.

His fingers reached into the sky and he began to spin. A blistering lead solo kept the fevered pace. Suddenly the music stopped — and so did Johnny. In his hands he cradled a ball of light.

He grinned at the audience as the orb grew brighter, revealing inside twinkling stars. The crowd cheered louder.

With a graceful toss, he sent the ball floating gently over his head. It sparkled as it caught the stage lights, glistening like a mirror ball, sailing through the air right toward Kara.

Kara recognized it instantly, the twinkling ball of stars with the bright silver glow in its center. She was looking at the fairy map. The gift from the Fairimentals to her. The one stolen last summer by the monstrous manticore.

Kara gazed at Johnny in fear. Then she felt the heat of the locket on her skin, and her thoughts began to get hazy again. In a burst of sudden panic, she tightened her grip on the unicorn horn.

But Johnny was no longer looking at her. His gaze was firmly fixed on the fairy map.

"Do what you have been destined for." His musical voice sounded like a chant. "You are the blazing star."

The fairy map began to settle around her, covering her in stars.

"Sing, Kara!" Johnny cried. "Make it happen."

The audience was on its feet breathlessly waiting to see what would follow this special effects extravaganza.

Kara struggled to fight Johnny's spell, to stop the song before it was too late. But she didn't have the strength. The unicorn horn could not protect her. She was just *another* falling star who had chosen the quick and easy path to achieving her dreams.

No! She *had* to fight this. "Lyra," she called out.

"*I'm here,*" the cat answered.

Kara started the next verse — but reaching out to her friend for strength she changed the words.

A web of lies spun so fast
I won't listen anymore
I can see through you at last,
Close the door, close the door, close the —

Suddenly, a chill wind kicked up and surrounded Johnny. In fury, he swung around and glared at Kara. What was that girl doing?

Kara tried to sing again, but she could barely catch her breath.

The crowd gasped. Her voice sounded horrible. She couldn't hit any of the notes.

"What's she doing?" Emily asked nervously.

"She's trying to change the words," Adriane said, surprised.

Kara's locket, the one Johnny had given her, was glowing white-hot, like a flame, making Kara cringe.

So *that* was what Johnny was using to control Kara!

Without a second thought, Adriane launched herself onstage. She ran to Kara and knocked the fairy map away from her. The ball floated gently over the crowd.

People in the audience started to bat it around, like a translucent beach ball.

Rage flared on Johnny's face, but only for a second. Dancing to the edge of the stage, he motioned for the crowd to send the ball back to him.

Adriane surged toward Kara, her hand reaching for the locket — but she was yanked back. A burly guard carried the struggling girl back to the wings.

A sudden, instinctive awareness flooded into Kara. The fairy map was always meant for her. Only she could sing the spell — to open it — and find Avalon.

She heard Johnny. "Kara, you are the blazing star — now *finish* the spell!"

Wide-eyed with horror, Kara realized the horrible mistake she'd made — all the wrong decisions and all the wrong ways she had used to justify them.

She felt herself spinning out of control, spiraling and turning inside out from the dark magic Johnny had worked on her.

She had to sing.

It was her dream.

Her *nightmare*.

There was a loud commotion backstage. Kara heard growls, scuffling, and people running. And then Adriane was before her, reaching for the locket. Kara had a flash that this was a mistake, the most terrible mistake anyone could make.

Or maybe that was just what Johnny wanted her to think.

Adriane's hand closed over the locket —

And for a single instant, Kara's and Adriane's minds were linked. In that instant, Kara understood that Adriane hadn't grabbed the locket for the sake of Ravenswood, or for Avalon, or even to protect herself; her only thought was to help her friend. Kara had been so wrong.

The chain securing the locket snapped — and Adriane threw it down, crushing it with her boot. Kara looked at Adriane, her eyes brimming with tears.

Adriane just nodded.

Howling with rage, Johnny ran around the stage, gesturing, and singing wildly.

The fairy map floated above the audience as they gently tapped it to and fro. Bright stars moved inside it in complex patterns.

If anyone had been out in the open field, they might have seen a much larger light show. Paths of stars swirled in the portal, creating a chain reaction of other portals opening, one by one, a frantic tumbling of cosmic dominoes.

Johnny sang and a swirling cloud of intense energy formed several feet above his head. Deep shades of red and blue blended together as bolts of lightning shot out from its center, reaching for the fairy map. Suddenly, something else bobbed up into the air above the audience. It swatted the fairy map away then fell back into the crowd.

"What was that?" Emily asked.

Some sort of furry animal was being tossed into the air above the heads of the crowd.

"Ozzie!" Emily cried.

"Whoo-hoo!" the ferret chortled as the crowd tossed him around. Each time Ozzie flew into the air, he swiped at the fairy map, knocking it further away from Johnny's grasp.

But all eyes were fixed on Kara, who was shining in a midnight-blue light that bathed the stage and the crowd.

She felt the blue fire of the horn engulfing her, burning away the very fabric of her being. Her star was going out in a blaze of glory.

Suddenly, a loud guitar chord barreled over the crowd. An enormous cheer rose up.

Adriane was standing beside Kara, guitar in hand. "Let's rock and roll!"

Together they sang, their voices mixing in magical harmony.

Together we stand
Able to do much more
Between us the power is ours,
Close the door, close the door, CLOSE THE DOOR!

Whirling around to signal his band, Johnny switched to another tune, his voice thundering out over the stage. Tossing his head back, he delivered a spellsong that released a blazing phoenix of red fire from the cloud above the stage. Adriane could feel its heat as it crackled and looked down at them, opening its maw as if to bake the girls where they stood.

Kara held the unicorn horn tight, and magic leaped forth. A blue-white unicorn made of clouds attacked the phoenix, impaling the fire creature with its horn. Cool silver sparkles rained down on the amazed audience as the images vanished.

Johnny turned to his band and launched into a smoldering version of the title song from his new CD.

I put a spell on you,
One look in my eyes, you know it's true
One note of my voice tells you what to do
Don't you know, I put a spell on you

Adriane's guitar squealed in feedback as sparks flew from it. The girls' voices faded as they began to sway under the spell of the song.

Suddenly, the sound of a flute sent a wondrous melody arcing over the crowd. It was Emily. She stood next to Kara and Adriane. Playing her flute, she sent out the song of Lorelei, the song of friendship she shared with the unicorn.

Johnny stopped singing. Was he weakening?

"Come on, girls," Kara yelled, "one for Be*Tween."

Kara, Adriane, and Emily sang together.

One chance for us all to stand together
One hope it's going to last forever
We've got the spirit
We're going to make it
I know we can
I know the magic's on our side

Kara's voice sounded like . . . Kara's voice, but to her friends it was the voice of an angel. Adriane and Emily joined in with perfect harmony.

"Everybody help us! Join in!" Kara called out.

The entire audience sang the chorus with the girls.

> *Don't wait for the sign*
> *It's one magic moment in time*
> *And you'll see through the haze*
> *One thousand lights will show you the way*
> *We've got the spirit*
> *We're going to make it*
> *I know the magic's on our side*
> *We've got the power in the darkest hour*
> *So don't give up the Spirit of Avalon*

Johnny was quivering, shimmering in lights. Be*Tween's song carried powerful magic. He ran behind the amplifiers as he began to lose his human form.

Kara saw a dark shadow and caught sight of a bat flying away from the stage. She stood between Adriane and Emily and held out her arms. Adriane and Emily held their wrists out and Kara touched each of their jewels. A bolt of magic flew from the gems, arcing out into the evening sky.

Fireworks lit up the night, as the Skultum was

ensnared in the magical blast. It was swept into the dreamcatcher and pulled into the swirling vortex. The portal closed.

For several long moments, there was nothing but silence on the great lawn of Ravenswood. Then someone in the audience started clapping and others joined in. The audience surged to its feet, crying out for more!

Kara embraced her friends as they took a bow to a thundering round of applause. The band was looking around uncertainly for Johnny.

Holding the mike, Kara announced, "Johnny had to fly. But before we go, I'd like to invite all the contest finalists to sing with us. Tonight, we're all stars!"

The excited girls and guys rushed onstage, surrounding Kara, Emily, and Adriane.

"I'd like our special animal friends to join us, too. They are the spirit of Ravenswood. Let's have a big hand for Stormbringer!"

The crowd cheered as the silver wolf loped onstage and stood next to Adriane.

"My best friend ever, Lyra!"

Lyra padded over to Kara. Kara knelt and hugged the cat so tightly, Lyra thought she would burst.

"Arial!" Emily shouted out.

The snow owl swooped over the astonished crowd and landed on Emily's arm.

Adriane took the mike. "And the one and only rock-and-roll ferret, Ozzie!"

The crowd went crazy cheering as Ozzie scampered onstage and took a bow.

Kara turned to Heather and smiled. "You start."

Heather smiled back and sang.

Nothing in this world can shake me
Trip me up or complicate me
Love is all that motivates me 'cause
I'm on a supernatural high

Everyone sang together. Their voices joined as one, sending the sweetest, truest, most powerful magic there was ringing out across the preserve, across their world, and across the magic web to what lay beyond. They sang from their hearts.

Chapter 14

"What were you thinking, Kara?" Adriane paced the floor of the library, throwing her arms in the air. "You and magic! It's like throwing gasoline on fire!"

Emily was there, too, next to Storm, Lyra, Ronif, and Balthazar. It had taken most of Sunday to get the great lawn cleaned up. It would still take some weeks before everything was back to normal. If that would ever be possible.

Kara nodded in agreement, eyes downcast, acting properly chagrined. She thought about how much she'd wanted to believe Johnny's lies, remembering the way she had almost given the Dark Sorceress the key to draw upon the power of Avalon itself. She had really messed up big time. Evil was easy, it provided shortcuts, instant rewards. Why was doing good so hard? But she already knew the answer. It sometimes involved sacrifice and wasn't always appreciated. And in the end, it was its own reward. Destruction was easy, building things that last was hard, like the friendships she had almost so carelessly thrown away. She leaned into Lyra, hugging her friend quietly.

The unicorn horn lay on the table where Kara had put it. Next to the crystal horn sat the glowing orb of stars, the tiny points of light inside configured in some still unknown pattern.

"We have retrieved the fairy map," Balthazar said. *"This is a major victory."*

"We haven't finished the 'I told you so's' yet," Adriane said, turning to the old pegasus.

"I've never seen so many messages," Ozzie called out. The ferret was at the computer, reading through hundreds of E-mails that had been pouring in from all over the world.

Best special effects we ever saw.

Congrats on a great show.

Are you available to appear in Springfield?

Ravenswood rules!

"Ha! Check this out," the ferret said. *"Teen singer Johnny Conrad rejoined his band in Memphis. When*

asked about the successful benefit performance at Ravenswood, he seemed in a daze and couldn't remember the show!"

Emily looked over the ferret's head. "Well, at least he's okay."

"Great!" Kara was on her feet. "The *real* Johnny Conrad won't remember anything!" she exclaimed sadly. Kara's star had come and gone.

"Here's one from the Town Council," Ozzie said.

Congratulations on a terrific event. Stone-hill has been on the news all day. The Parks Commission wants representatives to go to Washington. How about it, girls?

"Look out," Emily said. "Kara goes to Washington."

Kara hopped to her feet. "Tell them to send Mrs. Windor," she said, walking to the window.

The others stared at her.

"Let *her* take the credit. I've had my time in the spotlight," she said, staring wistfully out the window.

Emily glanced at Adriane and nudged her.

"Okay, okay," Adriane said. She reached into her backpack and lifted out a small box. "Face it, Barbie. You're a star, whether you like it or not." Kara stared at the dark-haired girl, then looked at the gift, a small smile appearing on her lips. "What's that?"

"We all wanted to get you something," Emily said. "So you would remember the concert and know that we will never forget what you have done."

"Thanks . . . but I wish I could forget what I did. You shouldn't have."

"Yeah, but we did anyway," Adriane said.

"I acted like such an idiot." Kara opened the box and removed a silver and gold band. And in the center was a small clasp ready to hold a stone — or jewel. "Wow. This is really nice!" Kara admitted truthfully.

"Read the inscription," Emily said, smiling.

To Kara,
Your star will always shine in our hearts.
Love, your friends at Ravenswood

"It's beautiful," Kara sniffled. She hugged Emily then turned to Adriane. "C'mon, you're next."

Adriane was about to protest but was caught in a hug.

"I know what the Fairimentals were trying to say to us," Kara said, turning to the group.

"What's that?" Adriane asked.

"They said, 'Spellsing as three.' Not one, but three. And that's what we did." Kara looked at all her friends. "We beat that monster by singing together, as three."

"We don't know what happened to the portals, whether they opened or not," Balthazar said, staring at the fairy map.

"Yes, but whatever the Sorceress tries next, she's got the *three* of us to deal with! Right, girls?" Kara held out her hand. Emily and Adriane stood strong and ready, jewels sparkling, hinting at concealed power.

"Right!" Emily put her hand on top of Kara's.

"Right!" Adriane put her hand on her friends' hands.

Sounds of music drifted from the computer monitor.

"Here's one!" Ozzie called out. The girls looked over the ferret's head at a bright icon arcing across the browser. It looked like a tiny shooting star.

"What kind of icon is that?" Adriane asked.

Ozzie clicked on the star. It was a file folder containing two messages. He opened the first.

Your concert was wonderful. We're sorry
we could not be there. We hope that until
we return, you will continue to spread
good magic with music. There is much to

be done. Music to heal, music to fire our passions, and music to blaze forever as inspirations of goodness. *Don't give up on the Spirit of Avalon.*
Your friends,
Be*Tween

"Be*Tween!" Kara said, amazed. "They know about the magic?"

Ozzie then opened the second message.

Your path has been opened, young mages. Now you must go forward, to-gether as three, and alone as a healer, a warrior, and a blazing star. It is time to walk your path . . . and come home. The magic is with you, now and forever.
Henry Gardener